THE THICK LINE

by

Jayne Gooding

BMP
Blue Mendos Publications

Published by Blue Mendos Publications
In association with Amazon KDP Publishing

Published in paperback 2022
Category: Crime Fiction
Copyright Jayne Gooding © 2022
ISBN : 9798849852096

Cover design by Jill Rinaldi © 2022

All rights reserved, Copyright under Berne Copyright Convention and Pan American Convention. No part of this book may be reproduced, stored in a retrieval system, or transmitted in any form or by any means, electronic, mechanical, photocopying, recording or otherwise, without prior permission of the author. The author's moral rights have been asserted.

This is a work of fiction. Names, characters, corporations, institutions, organisations, events or locales in this novel are either the product of the author's imagination or, if real, used fictitiously. Any resemblance to actual persons (living or dead) is entirely coincidental.

Dedication

For my Mum. Many people don't believe in love at first sight, but I loved you Mum from the day I was born.

My good friend and mentor, the late Marky Mark who, when I needed it most, ran a long-distance cross country run, barefoot, to motivate and support me. One of the kindest and closest friends I've ever had.

To my cousin and friend Gillian Aghajan for all her support and hard work during the processing of this book.

Chapter 1

⬅———————➡

Bristol 1976

The Ford Escort police car was parked under the streetlight alongside a parade of shops and opposite The Tropicana Nightclub. It was 11 pm and the clubbers would be leaving in the next few hours. On Thursdays the club's occupants would leave without too much trouble. Fridays and Saturdays after a night of heavy drinking were different. It would be carnage with arguments, fights and public disorder.

Constable Steve Robinson closed his eyes and slowly exhaled, leaving his King Size Rothman cigarette smoke to drift out through his nostrils and into the cold night air. He glanced around the empty street before stubbing the butt out into the car's ash tray. He rolled up the window and turned to WPC Lucy Penfold.

"So, what's the story between you and PC Boyce? It seemed like one minute you guys are paired up on patrol and the next, well the next you're teamed with me."

"I don't know." replied Lucy. "Maybe because I am the token female on the section the Sergeant allocates me to different crewmates on different nights. I guess he is easing me in to integration and allowing me to meet all of the members of the section slowly, and them to meet and work with me. It's only been a few months since integration has been fully implemented with women on patrol, so I guess we are all getting used to it. I have to say though, I am thoroughly happy to be working with the men. The work is so much more varied and exciting!"

"I thought there was more to it than that. I did ask around before we teamed up, but no one seemed to know anything." said PC Robinson, chuckling.

"If you're insinuating that there was romantic indiscretion then I'm sorry to disappoint you, because you're mistaken. I have only been out with PC Boyce a few nights...I don't know what else to tell you."

"How did you get on with our 'Neanderthal' PC Boyce? He's a bit of an animal isn't he?" said PC Robinson.

Lucy thought carefully about her reply and merely said, "Oh, he's okay."

Lucy's mind shifted back to the night before, when she was on night patrol with PC Boyce. He was a scruffy looking officer. Lucy had noticed his shirt wasn't starched and pressed like the other male officers' shirts and his shoes were dirty. She thought him brash and unprofessional in his approach to the public and police work. Every time she had been in the car with him he had insisted on driving for the first part of the night, then he would give her the keys at about 3am, get into the passenger seat, put his feet on the dashboard, pull his police cap down over his eyes and promptly fall asleep.

Lucy remembered with disgust how he had lifted the cheeks of his bottom off the seat and farted loudly, asking her if she knew what flavour curry he had eaten that evening.

Lucy was not used to such behaviour. He had also done it on the previous night that she had been crewed with him. Lucy had asked him not to do it then, this second time she had said to him, "Look, will you stop doing that, it is downright disgusting and I am a captive audience here! I have already asked you nicely not to do it, now I am telling you!"

PC Boyce just laughed and said, "Get over yourself!" Then with a real mean look on his face he said, "You wanted to join the Police Force, we didn't ask you to. Now I have to not only think about protecting myself when the going gets tough, I have to protect you as well! You get the same pay as us now, and I have to babysit you, it doesn't seem right to me. This is a man's world, you're in my space and if I want to fart I will. As far as I am concerned, women are here to be used and abused."

Lucy could feel herself getting annoyed, but she said calmly, "PC Boyce, understand this, you will never use and abuse me. I am not putting up with your antics and that's a fact. If you fart in my company again, I can assure you I will take steps to make sure it is the last time."

"Oh yeah?" PC Boyce said with a sneer. "What exactly are you going to do about it?"

"Wait and see," said Lucy. She instantly realised that there was little she could do about it, there was no one to tell. If she told a Senior Officer she would be labelled a 'tell-tale'; if she told one of her male colleagues it would be around the station within minutes. There was no formal mechanism in place for complaints of this nature; the men would probably just laugh at her, and she could be ostracised. Still, she had thrown down the gauntlet and wondered if he would dare to pick it up.

The question was quickly answered. PC Boyce said, "Whoops, here comes another one and it's gonna be big!" With that he let rip an almighty, smelly fart.

Immediately afterwards a lost looking member of the public knocked on the car window. Lucy opened it and a man leaned forward into the car, ignoring Lucy, seemingly intent on only speaking to the male officer. He was holding a piece of paper and then he moved sharply back, grasping his nose and repeatedly saying, "Oh my god, Oh my god!"

Lucy got out of the car and went over to the man. She had said, "Let me help you with that," and taking the piece of paper from him, she gave him directions to where he was going. She remembered being so embarrassed and just getting back into the patrol car asking PC Boyce to drive off.

At 3am, PC Boyce pulled up to the kerb and turned off the ignition. Barely a word had passed between them since that last fart, as Lucy was still shocked and annoyed. She got into the driver's seat and drove, whilst PC Boyce put his feet up on the dashboard and fell asleep as usual.

It was a quiet little town, and it was winter. Hardly anything moved or happened for the police to get involved in, so Lucy had driven around looking for stolen vehicles and checking Industrial properties. Suddenly an idea came to her. She drove out to the limit of her beat, a small seaside village, where she knew there was a car park. She drove into the car park and saw one lone vehicle parked in the corner. Lucy shook PC Boyce awake and excitedly said, "Look a stolen vehicle!" She pointed at the lone car parked under a tree. "Quickly PC Boyce, jump out and see if the engine is warm. I will do a radio check on it".

PC Boyce woke up with a shock and said, "How do you know it's stolen?"

Lucy replied, "I have a photographic memory. I recognise the number plate. Quickly go feel if the engine is warm!"

PC Boyce opened the passenger door and egressed with the speed of a striking slug, he walked slowly over to the vehicle and ducked down to see if there was anyone in it.

Lucy saw her chance and drove away, leaving PC Boyce in the car park. As she turned the car around, she shouted out the window to him, "Bye, enjoy your walk back to the nick. You must learn,

when you fart in my presence there will always be dire consequences!" and waved as she left the car park.

It was normal for vehicles to return to the station between 4 and 4.30 am and officers enjoyed a quick tea break, courtesy of the newest 'sprog' on section, whose duties including making the section tea. Tea making was seen as a way to endear yourself to the section, and a good 'sprog' would take careful note and prepare lists of how each section member liked their tea or coffee, with or without milk or sugar.

Lucy pulled into the station yard and went for her quick cuppa. The Sergeant saw her walking alone into the work kitchen. "Where is PC Boyce?" he asked her.

Lucy had told him that PC Boyce wanted to stretch his legs and do a bit of foot patrol, but that he would be back at 6am at the conclusion of his duty. The Sergeant had scratched his head, looked in disbelief and said, "Hmmm ok then."

At about 5.45am PC Boyce arrived on foot back at the station. He was red faced and very angry. He walked straight into Lucy, who was in the front office returning a bottle of Tipp-Ex to the drawer after typing out a report.

"How dare you abandon me in the middle of nowhere!" PC Boyce shrieked.

"How dare you fart in the car every time I am on patrol with you," Lucy had replied.

"You wait!" said PC Boyce almost spitting his words. "I am going to report you to the Superintendent for this!"

"Go for it!" said Lucy, "When he calls me to his office to see me, I will explain to him EXACTLY why I have had to resort to such an action and we will see who comes off best!"

Lucy went on to tell him that she had warned him and he only had himself to blame, and then she went off duty.

***

Lucy was delighted to return to work the following night to find she had been crewed with PC Robinson.

"Lucy, answer me, what is OK about him?" laughed PC Robinson. "Uh," said Lucy, "what do you mean?"

I asked you what was OK about PC Boyce and you went into a world of your own Lucy. Earth to Lucy, come in please," he mocked.

"Oh I am just tired," replied Lucy, "I will be glad to finish this week of night shifts and that's a fact," and she let out a long yawn.

Lucy realised that she liked PC Robinson, he was fun to be crewed with and had a pleasant gentlemanly manner to him.

***

A man staggered out from the KFC fast food chicken take-away door entrance. He was about six feet tall with long, wild, bleached blonde hair and a gold cross earring hanging from his left ear. He wore an orange coloured tank top with blue, faded denim jeans and scruffy, brown platform boots. He had the appearance of an aged glam rock pop star who had been on a three-day drink, drugs and cheap hooker binge.

The officers watched him trip and recover several times but still manage to stay on his feet with the fast food box firmly in his hand. As he passed the police car, he stopped and stared at Lucy for several seconds before shooting a V sign with his fingers and shouting, "Fuck off copper!"

"What!" said PC Robinson in disbelief.

"Leave it," Lucy said in a calm almost pleading voice, "he's just drunk."

Again, the drunken Rocker threw a V sign and shouted, "Yes that's right, fuck off coppers!"

"I'm not having this," said PC Robinson. "That kind of language should not be used in front of ladies."

"Really, it's okay. He'll be on his sweet merry way and have no memory of this in the morning," said Lucy.

Constable Robinson paused for a moment, "I don't care Lucy I'm going to have a word," and then stepped out the car.

"Excuse me sir but that kind of language or behaviour is not acceptable."

The Rocker staggered back. He towered over the Constable. Looking him up and down he puffed out his chest and with a drunken manic grin said, "Well you can fuck off as well PC Plod!"

Lucy got out the car.

"I'm warning you sir," continued Constable Robinson sternly, "that any more of this and you will be arrested for being drunk and disorderly."

The Rocker drunkenly rubbed his unshaven chin and spoke. "Allow me to retort sir. I may be shitfaced and drunk but you cunt...stable are short and ugly, however tomorrow I'll be sober and you will still be a short arse with a face that looks like it should be fed a banana."

"Please sir," said Lucy motioning him away, "can you please just curb the language and make your way home like a good citizen."

Looking Lucy up and down the rocker sneered. "I can't say I think much of your uniform darling. Why don't you slip into something else... like a coma?"

Constable Robinson was agitated, frustrated and out of patience. He reached for his £5 hand cuffs purchased from The Police Review magazine and attempted to grab the Rocker's wrist.

The Rocker brushed it away dropping his prized KFC box. "Now look what you made me do. That was my fucking dinner. I had drumsticks, fries and everything. I should bloody well slap you, but then again shit stains."

The Constable sucked on his teeth noisily and made a second attempt for the Rocker's arm. He missed and stumbled on the cracked pavement, falling to his knees.

"Do you know what copper, there must be a village out there desperately missing their idiot," the Rocker hissed.

The officer scrambled back to his feet and lunged again for the Rocker's wrist.

"Fuck off!" the Rocker bellowed. The fury in his voice was almost tangible. His left arm fired a punch that just missed its target. He fired again and again, each time missing the Constable's weaving and bobbing head. With both hands free the Rocker ran forward with his fists and boots shooting and kicking wildly in all directions. The Constable stepped backwards and fell onto his backside by the kerb.

Lucy was a slim build but almost six foot tall and had received some training in martial arts, which she had relished. Stepping forward she seized the Rocker side on and threw him over her hip. As he took to the air he grabbed Lucy's jacket and they both ended up sprawled across the road. She found herself lying between his legs. Constable Robinson dived across them both, but the Rocker wouldn't stay still. His body, arms and legs thrashed around like an eel in the bottom of a bucket.

Two further policemen, who were out on foot patrol, spotted the disturbance and ran to give assistance to their fellow officers. The crazed Rocker was relentless, running on neat alcohol and adrenalin. He pushed, punched and kicked out at all four officers. He refused to submit.

Seconds later a dark blue Rover V8 police car screeched to a halt and both occupants, with truncheons in hand, joined the scuffle. Lucy was still placed between the Rocker's legs. She had narrowly missed his kicking and was still pinned down by the body parts of her fellow officers. Lucy head was near his groin. This had to stop before somebody got seriously hurt. She was being suffocated, struggling for breath. She opened her mouth and lunged forward, and without knowing it, bit down hard on the Rocker's testicles. He let out an ear-piercing scream, but believing it was his leg, Lucy just bit down harder refusing to let go until the body stopped all movement.

In seconds the Rocker was handcuffed, on his feet and scuffled into the back of the police car, his head buried into his lap wincing with pain, and crying uncontrollably.

In the custody suite, a Senior Officer seeing the disarray of the arriving police officers and their prisoner asked, "Are you okay WPC Penfold?"

"Yes Sir," she answered brushing herself down. "I'm fine now thank you."

"Well done officer," he said with a discreet grin, "very well done."

Lucy nodded, "Thank you, Sir."

"Hey", called out Constable Robinson with a smile. "I don't think the criminals or anyone back at the nick, for that matter, will be in a hurry to mess with you WPC Testicle Biter!"

Chapter 2

One year earlier: England, the South West 1975

Lucy had been collected from her home by Laura, Clare and Karen; they were all new police recruits and were travelling together to Cwmbran Police Training College in South Wales. They had all met, albeit briefly, at the recruitment centre. There had been thirty people interviewed that day, of which sixteen were cadets and already promised entry. Another thirteen had sufficient qualifications to pass on to the next stage.

Lucy didn't favour dresses so had arrived in her brown, French cut trousers, pink pastel coloured linen jacket from Marks & Spencer's which had the sleeves turned, and a pretty, candy striped blouse in white, pink and brown. She had worn flat shoes because she was tall.

Sergeant Smith had commented on how quiet she was. "I'm just a little shy Sir," she replied.

Lucy was led through to a large empty room with wooden flooring. There was a large carved crest on a rostrum and a clock.

The Sergeant tried to put her at ease. "Don't be put off by me or the place. You will have three test papers which will include observations. Whatever happens you must try and finish within the allotted time."

Lucy took a deep breath with an awkward smile and sat down. Following a nod from the Sergeant she began reading the papers hungrily.

Waiting alone in the hallway for her results Lucy spotted the Sergeant walking briskly towards her.

"I'm stunned, Miss Penfold, never before in history of this centre has anyone ever, and I do mean ever, passed all three exam papers with a hundred per cent score. Well done!"

Lucy looked up at the Sergeant and blushed, "Thank you Sir."

"The next stage will be easy now. There's a woman Superintendent on site who will interview you," he smiled and shrugged his shoulders. "Now unless you tell her to bugger off or insult her parents, you will be going into the force at the best point in police history. We've just had the biggest pay rise ever and you as a WPC will get equal pay."

Lucy had passed her medical, entrance exams and been given a start date. She had achieved what to her was the unachievable. They had issued her with a small brown case filled with her uniform. Lucy left the centre, looked up to the cloudy sky above and punched the air screaming out "YES!!!!"

***

Karen twiddled with the radio knobs as the reception began fading. She found Radio 1 which had the song 'Barbados by Typically Tropical' playing.

"I love this track," said Laura.

"Me too," agreed Karen, "turn it up."

"Wooo I'm going to Cwmbran," sang Laura. "Wooo gonna join the police force."

The other girls began laughing out loud and joined in.

"Wooo I'm going to Cwmbran, wooo gonna join the police force."

"Hey look there's a pub," Laura pointed. "Shall we stop off for lunch? We're making good time."

It was a glorious sunny day, so the girls sat outside in the garden with their ploughman's lunches and cokes.

Laura was slim; very pretty with very long, blonde hair that had been made up into pigtails. Every inch of her being oozed sex appeal. Clare was a little overweight and had commented several times about her being on a diet and yet ordered two packets of salt and vinegar crisps with her lunch. It had made Lucy smile as she glanced down at Clare's bulging waistline.

"So," said Laura taking the lead," what's your story, why are you here? What made you want to join the police force?"

"That's easy," answered Clare. "Our family grew up around watching police shows like Dixon of Dock Green and Z cars. I suppose I always knew that one day I'd be a policewoman. What about you?"

Karen looked around at each of the girls, took a deep breath and began. "My family has a long history with the police. My father, grandfather and uncles are all in the force. My brother Billy followed in the family footsteps. I can remember how proud everyone was of him when he returned home with his case and uniform. My father organised a big party when training finished, and he received his first posting. It was a big affair at a big posh hotel with waiters, champagne and everything. I was only a little girl, but I remember how happy everyone was."

"Where is your brother stationed? " asked Laura.

"He was given a posting in London. He had always wanted to be in The Met even as a little boy. Billy loved the idea of catching proper villains like the Kray Twins or The Richardsons. So, he volunteered for everything and anything. My brother Billy was always the first in with dreams of medals and making the world a safer place. Then while out on foot patrol he spotted a car racing towards him with police cars hot on its tail, with the lights and sirens on. Billy drew his truncheon and strode out into the road and stood there with his arm out and his truncheon held up high. The car didn't stop and ploughed straight into my brother. He died on the way to hospital. The villains were never caught. Billy was killed for a pitiful £1200 that had been robbed from a security van. The family was heartbroken, my mother cried for weeks. I don't think she ever truly got over it. So, I decided that I would join for my brother Billy. I would carry on where he left off and bring pride and happiness back to the family."

The girls sat in an embarrassed silence for a few seconds.

"Wow that is deep Karen, I'm so sorry for your loss. I'm sure we all are," volunteered Lucy.

"Your turn Lucy," said Karen perking up and wiping away a tear.

"No, not me yet. Let's hear Laura".

"Yeah come on Laura, what's your story?" said everyone in unison.

Laura applied her rouge lipstick, pouted her plumped shapely lips and gave a beaming white smile; "I suppose it's because of men really. I don't know why but whenever I'm going out with someone and it starts getting serious there's this expectation. You know what I mean girls? Talk about getting married, kids and well, all I could see was an image of my mum stuck in the kitchen cooking and cleaning up after everyone. My dad just coming home from work, plonked down in the chair still in his dirty overalls with the TV on and my Mum bringing him a glass of Brown Ale and his dinner. She always looked so, well worn out almost resigned to her lot. I didn't want that, I needed something different. Maybe just the fun side of a relationship, like going out with friends, laughing and flirting harmlessly with the good-looking lads," she winked.

"So, you joined the police to not become a wife?" quizzed Clare.

Laura continued, "It was a little bit more than that. There was this good looking lad; clean clear skin, gleaming white teeth and his hair was cut and styled like David Cassidy. If you stood Tony next to David Cassidy, you would be hard pressed to tell them apart. Tony and I had been going out together on and off since school. He'd look at me with those big blue eyes, wink and I'd just melt. He was the first one who I had ever done anything with, if you know what I mean. Not the full thing, you know the business or anything, but I did let him touch me. He was special not like the other lads, there was always something more about him. Well things progressed and together we became more heated in our playing around together and Tony wanted more. He told me about there being free contraception available for women. Reluctantly I agreed. It wasn't that I didn't love or want to sleep with him. I just didn't feel ready. Well I did anyway. It happened, and we became lovers. I'd be lying if I said there were fireworks, there wasn't. It was pain and discomfort followed by a few minutes of heavy breathing and bingo, all over.

Everything changed after that. Tony changed towards me. He became jealous if someone looked at me and boy, would he go crazy if someone spoke to me. It became difficult going out, especially if there were other boys there. I tried speaking to him about it, telling him that there was no need to be jealous and that we were together. Okay he said, let's get married. I was shocked. I said that I'd think about it and eventually said maybe, in a few years, when we were both a little older and settled in jobs with a regular income. Tony wasn't happy and began going out to the pub and drinking heavily. That's when he'd get argumentative and start fighting.

He'd come around to my house with a bloody nose expecting me to patch him up. The conversation always turned to he wouldn't have been out drinking if we were married and that somehow it was my fault that his life had taken a turn for the worse. It did all come to an end one Friday night. It was my birthday and I'd gone out to have a few drinks with friends. I was having a great time, just girly fun when Tony arrived at the pub. He was drunk, really drunk and had a face like thunder when he saw me talking innocently to a guy from work. The next thing I knew Tony pushed me to the floor, picked up a light ale bottle and smashed it across the lad's head. The lad collapsed to the floor with blood oozing out all over the carpet. My friends began to scream, some ran from the bar. Tony just stood over me with his fists clenched and through gritted teeth told me that this was my fault and look what I had made him do. The landlord was ex- army and grabbed Tony from behind and wrestled him to the floor. It wasn't long before the police arrived.

I'll always remember the officer had a WPC with him. She was great; she calmed people and helped to take names of witnesses. For the first time, probably in my life, I had absolute clarity. I wanted independence, to make my own choices and not follow my mum, my family or just about every female that I'd ever met. I decided to make use of my qualifications and become a policewoman."

"Well done, good for you," said Clare.

Slowly shaking her head in disbelief Lucy stated, "You are one very brave lady."

"You sure are," said Karen. "Why is it that men have to be such bastards? I don't mean all men obviously but why do they feel the need to own you after being intimate? That's not loving or caring about your girlfriend. I don't know, but stuff like that just makes me angry. Anyway, we're all pleased that you're out of that relationship Laura and here en route to a new exciting adventure."

"Thank you," Laura smiled and blew a mock kiss. "Right, now it's your turn Lucy."

All the girls turned to face her, eyes wide with anticipation. Clare ate the last of the groups' pickled onions.

"This is difficult after hearing your stories. For me it was no more than seeing an advert in the newspaper and applying. It really wasn't any more than that."

"Sometimes that's all it ever is, "said Laura. "Destiny can just change the path of our lives. Anyway," she looked at her watch, "we have got to get going. We don't want to be late on our first day."

Lucy gave an inner sigh of relief. She hadn't had to share the truth, the real reason that she sat among them. That was her business, it wasn't for the public domain. She refused to let the past or her environment dictate who and what she would become.

To the outside world Lucy's parents were no different from many of the neighbours in her road. Dad was a long distance lorry driver and was away a lot, but he made time for the children when he was at home. His wife, Lucy's mother, Charlotte was the centre of his universe. She was a stunning woman with her big brown eyes, wavy blonde hair and long shapely legs. Her voluptuous curves turned heads wherever she went but she only had eyes for her husband.

Even from an early age Lucy's mum interacted differently to her brother and sister. Lucy rarely had new clothes bought for her but was forced to wear mother's old tops, over-sized shoes or skirts that she no longer wore. The clothes would hang awkwardly from Lucy's slim childlike frame. Her friends had stopped knocking for her to come out and play having been refused so many times at the front door. Lucy would sit in her room and stare out the window at the happy children playing and ask herself what she had done for her mum to be so hard with her and not her siblings. They would carry on their business about the house with no interference and yet mother's eyes were on her the second she entered the room.

When Lucy tried to make conversation about something she had done at school there was rarely more than a grunt or nod. At ten years old she was promised a bike if she passed her eleven plus exam at school. Lucy had an incredible gift, a photographic memory. She discovered this at an early age and could visualise things that she had read or seen written on the classroom blackboard. Passing tests had not been difficult; she had excelled with maximum marks. The teacher had proudly given her a letter to take home. Lucy had been so excited; she wanted the bike she'd been promised. Her little legs could almost feel themselves pushing the peddles and racing around the park with her friends. She bounded excitedly through the door with the letter grasped between her fingers. Her face could hardly disguise her excitement. Her mother took the letter and placed it on the mantelpiece over the open fire. Lucy had asked if she was going to read it. "Yes, yes, maybe later," had been the answer with almost indifference. Dinner came and went and again Lucy asked for the letter to be read. Eventually her mum picked it up, read its contents and then turned to Lucy. "So, who did you sit next to at school? I want to know who you stole the answers from."

Lucy was shocked and disappointed, "No one mummy, no one. I did it all on my own. I worked hard so that you would get me my bike."

Her mother replied, "I do not believe you. You are a stupid girl and certainly not smart enough to have passed the eleven plus on your own. No, you cheated and of that I'm sure. There will be no bike and I may have to go to the school and tell them what a liar and cheat you are."

"That's not true mummy, honest. I did it all on my own."

***

Lucy never got her bike despite her pleas and confirmation from her school teachers that she was an exceptionally bright student. Lucy had tried to argue that a bike should not have been promised if there was never an intention to buy it for her. Eventually her mother came home with a second-hand Spirograph set and she was told to make do. Lucy hated it. She wanted to be out riding on a new bike with her friends not sitting at a table with a pencil and bits of plastic cogs making patterns. She purposely took pieces of the set and placed them in the dirt by the washing line. It was a silent protest; she knew her mother would see them.

Dressed in an ex-student's second-hand school uniform, Lucy went to the local Grammar School and quickly became an A- grade student. When she was almost 15 she was told that she'd been kept for the last fourteen years and now it was her turn to go out and get a job. She was to make a financial contribution to the household. It had been difficult as there were no real jobs for someone of her age so again her mother took her by the arm and frog marched her down to the secretarial college. It was not what Lucy wanted; she had no ambitions to sit in a typing pool. She felt there was more for her. The fellow students were all three or four years older than Lucy but still she kept on making top marks and outperformed all her peers.

Lucy passed all her advanced typing classes and again raced home to tell her mum, who said, "I don't believe you. You're stupid! I told you before and I'll tell you again you're just stupid."

***

Lucy got her first job in a typing pool. The pay was eleven pounds per week. Her mother demanded eight pounds as they were struggling to keep up the mortgage payments. Even when Lucy bought an item of new clothing her mum would tell her it'd looked better on her and confiscated it. The only way Lucy could stay ahead was to buy two items of identical clothing. When the company began to lay people off Lucy found herself out of a job. Mother very quickly organised interviews at the local banks and drove Lucy to them so there was to be no escape. At each bank Lucy looked around at the employees; these were stuffy environments and not for her. At each interview Lucy calmly and politely told the Manager that she really didn't feel that office work was for her, and convinced the manager to provide a cup of tea in another office so that her mum, who was waiting in the car outside, would be none the wiser.

Eventually Lucy ran out of options and her mother drove her to a secretarial agency and sat with her whilst she filled in the necessary forms. Lucy was never given an opportunity to choose her occupation; it didn't seem to matter what she wanted to do, so she joined the agency and was placed on a week's typing role in a local factory. The pay was thirteen pounds per week and again her mother took eight pounds on pay day. The placement continued for almost fourteen weeks but was several miles away and because she didn't have enough money for buses, clothes and lunch she would leave the house early and walk and not arrive home until late. It was worse when it rained. There were times when she had to skip meals, so she could buy stockings. On many occasions she sat on the bench outside the factory feeling desperately hungry whilst her friends and colleagues bought fish and chips.

Lucy pleaded with her mum that she was just taking too much if her earnings. She couldn't eat, buy clothes and the long walk made her tired. Her desperate pleas fell on deaf, indifferent ears. Mother wanted that eight pounds and nothing would change that.

***

The placement finally came to an end. Lucy was almost distraught. Although her manager was pleased with her work, the company had already kept her beyond the week originally required. She dreaded going home and telling Mother her bad news.

For the following few weeks Lucy left the home, as normal, and sat outside the factory. She waited for her friends to come out at lunch time. They would buy her chips and chat. Lucy asked them to please let her know if anything, absolutely anything became available in the factory. On Fridays she would give her mother eight pounds from her savings, but by now Lucy was getting desperate, her savings were meagre and would not last for another week. Finally, one of her friends handed her a card with a job. It hadn't even been put in the local newspaper yet or on the wall at work. Lucy didn't hesitate. She phoned from the call box opposite the factory and made an appointment to meet the department manager Mr Stephen Ross the following day.

The card read that it would be a secretary's role with typing skills to Pitman level 2, shorthand seventy words per minute and the role would include running errands. Applicants must be over thirty years of age.

Lucy knew this would be a challenge. She was seventeen and looked fifteen but she had a plan.

Stephen Ross was a handsome man. He smiled and welcomed Lucy into his office and showed her the chair. There was some small talk about travelling and Lucy noticed the photograph of him with his wife and family. She sensed that part of the job specification was because his wife would not want him working with a potential dolly bird. Lucy would have to take the lead and start the real interview.

"Mr Ross, I know that the card asked for someone of thirty or above but I believe the benefit of employing someone like me is that this would be my first role as a secretary. I do not have any of the bad habits that could be picked up over the years elsewhere. I will seek to understand what you need and deliver it. Someone over thirty may have had one boss for many years and they expect you then to work around how they know the role. Mr Ross, I am trustworthy, honest, loyal and very hardworking. I do not watch the clock. If we must work late then I'll be here until you tell me the task is complete." She paused for a second, "I really want this job."

"I'm not sure," Stephen stuttered, "what qualifications do you have?"

Lucy smiled enthusiastically. "Mr Ross, I have a Pitman Level 3 qualification and my Pitman's shorthand is ninety words per minute, so I am actually more qualified than you have advertised for."

Stephen was taken aback, he reached across his desk for the ashtray. He moved his papers and opened his desk drawer. "Did you happen to see my cigarettes and lighter?" he said.

"Not in here, but whilst I was waiting to see you I did see a packet of ten Woodbines with a gold lighter on a table in the canteen earlier, and a woman sitting at the table who didn't seem interested in them."

"Okay, I'm just going to pop out and get them. I won't be a minute."

A few minutes later Stephen returned shaking his head. "Someone must have picked them up."

Lucy said, "Well the woman I saw sitting at the same table was wearing a pleated, black knee length skirt, black stockings and heels. Her jacket was red with gold buttons. I would say she must have been about five feet seven inches tall, with dark brown, shoulder length hair and she wore glasses for reading."

Stephen's eyes lit up in amazement. "That sounds like Sandra from personnel. Two minutes, I'll just give her quick ring."

Stephen placed the phone back on the hook. "It was Sandra, she saw them and picked them up for me. Lucy I am amazed how could you remember such details?"

"I have a photographic memory Mr Ross. I see things once and just remember everything."

"Well Lucy Penfold I'm going to do something I've never done before," he smiled. "I'd like to offer you the job. Can you start tomorrow?"

Lucy beamed, "You will not regret this Mr Ross."

***

The pay was thirty six pounds per month but Lucy's mother wanted thirty two. There was no reasoning. It was then that she started calling Stephen Ross at work and telling him that Lucy had to earn more if she were to continue working with him. It had been very embarrassing for them both, but Stephen liked Lucy and was very happy with her work. He avoided her mother's phone calls with excuses that he was out the office or away on business. He explained to Lucy that the job couldn't pay any more, but he would allow her to work Saturday mornings to earn some extra cash as overtime.

As she got older her friends asked her to join them out on Friday or Saturday nights at the pub in town, and she usually spent her Sunday with her best friend Gillian. On one occasion she had got ready and was waiting anxiously for Gillian to call. Lucy stepped out into the garden to say goodbye to her mother, who was pegging out washing, and was completely taken by surprise when her mother told her that she had invited two young cousins to visit and that Lucy was required to stay in and keep them entertained. Lucy tried to explain that she had made prior arrangements and was just about to leave to meet Gillian so she was unable to stay, but her mother was adamant. Lucy went back into the kitchen and sat at the table waiting for her friend Gillian to call. She felt a dripping sensation and then stood up as brown liquid covered her dress. Her mother had taken a full pot of stale cold tea and poured it all over head. She then grabbed Lucy by the arm and dragged her to the front door and threw her out onto the pathway, locking the kitchen door in her face.

As Lucy sat on the concrete slab soaked in a puddle of tea and leaves she had an epiphany. She would leave the family home and her mother today.

About fifteen minutes later the door was unlocked, Lucy walked past her mother, up the stairs and washed her hair. She then filled a carrier bag with what little clothes she had, together with a small transistor radio that had been given to her as a present for her birthday and walked downstairs with a mission to accomplish.

"Where are you going?" her mother demanded.

"I'm leaving here and leaving you," replied Lucy her voice trembling full of anger.

"Why don't you sit down and we can talk about this over a nice cup of tea?" her mother said.

"No thank you, I've just had a pot full," Lucy sneered.

Lucy brushed past her mother and out of the front door. Enraged by not getting her own way, her mother marched up to the front gate and called out up the road, "Don't you dare go to my mother's!"

Lucy held back the tears, the lump in her throat was choking and made it difficult for her to breath.

***

Brenda was one of the bosses at the factory. She and Lucy had become good friends. Brenda was single and lived alone several miles away. Lucy had no money for a taxi so began walking. It was late before Brenda arrived home with her sister and two merry sailors.

"What are you doing here Lucy, is everything alright?"

Lucy stood up from the door step and explained her problem and asked if she could stay for a few days to get herself sorted with a flat. Brenda beckoned her in, "Of course you can, good for you Lucy. I'll help you as much as I can."

***

It wasn't long before mother was back on the phone to Stephen Ross only this time asking him to relay messages. She told him that Lucy's clothes would be taken outside and burned in the garden if they were not collected by 4pm that afternoon. It wasn't possible because Lucy was still working. Mother phoned at 4pm right on the dot saying to Stephen, "I want you to tell her that I want her home now!"

Lucy took the phone and said calmly that she wouldn't be coming back and hung up the receiver.

"Listen Lucy," said Stephen, "I'll get Barry to run you home, so you can get your belongings. If that woman starts anything then you come straight back here."

Later that afternoon Lucy read some papers that had been left on the table in the canteen. It was recruitment information for men and woman to join the police force. This could be my escape route Lucy told herself. She photocopied the application form, filled it in and posted it out the same day.

Lucy decided she had to stay at her mother's, as she was making life difficult for her at work and had even contacted a potential landlord. Lucy would do what she had to do until she knew if the police force was an option or not.

***

Following the application, a Woman Inspector arrived at the house. It was standard practice for applicants to be thoroughly vetted. Mother answered the door.

"Hello, does Lucy live here?" asked the Inspector.

"Yes, but you can't come in. She will not be joining the police."

"Oh, I see. Do you not like the police Mrs Penfold?"

"No," she stuttered, "it's not that. I forbid Lucy to join the police force."

"Mum really, I'm eighteen years old and I can make my own mind up about what I want to do with my life." Lucy's tone was calm and self-assured.

"Lucy," her mother bellowed, whilst shaking her pointing finger, "why did you apply? You are not bright enough! You are stupid, you will do as you're told!"

"That's a real shame Mrs Penfold," said the Inspector calmly. "I really have come a long way. Would you mind if I had a cup of tea?"

"Okay come in, but it will need to be quick because we have things to do," Mother snapped back.

As Mother left the room the Inspector whispered, "Lucy, I'll send you the details for your interview."

***

After Lucy had passed all her entry exams and had been issued with her uniform and start date she wanted to run home and share her good news. As they sat at the family dinner table Lucy dropped in conversation that she had received a letter from the police. She waited and waited but there was no question of what or why, so she stayed quiet.

From then until the morning she was due to leave Lucy said nothing. On that final day she came downstairs with her case, thinking about what Stephen Ross had told her when she gave her notice. There had been a company intelligence test a few weeks before and he had the results. Lucy had scored amongst the highest in the company including some of the most senior managers. He told her that he would miss her but wished her every success with her new career. Her thoughts were interrupted.

"Where are you going?" demanded her mother. "To join the police," was Lucy's abrupt answer. "You never told me."

"No mother you never asked so I didn't tell."

"Well what about your breakfast?"

"I don't want any breakfast."

"Well then young lady, know this. If you walk outside that front door you will never be coming back!"

"Okay," Lucy's expression now completely indifferent, "good bye Mum."

***

The girls finished their pub lunch and climbed back into Laura's gold Ford Cortina 1600E.

Chapter 3

"**R**ight you lot!" bellowed the Drill Sergeant "Fall in Line!"

Lucy and the girls had arrived at the training college and were quickly allocated rooms within the six blocks, all of which housed thirty officers. Lucy and Clare had been given single quarters whilst Karen and Laura were in the dormitory. Lucy's room was white and small with a green carpet. It had a single bed with a duvet which was a pleasant surprise, because she'd never seen one before. It was furnished with a wooden chair, desk and bedside table. She had been given a coffee mug, towel and a glass ash tray with strict instructions that no more than three items could be left out on display in her room at any given time, and that rooms would be subject to inspection without notice.

On arrival all the officer trainees had been asked to line up on the parade ground, where they were told of the regulation haircut. Men had to have short back and sides. If a woman's hair was short, then it had to be cut really short at the back and off the collar. However, if it was long, like Lucy's and Laura's then it was fine, as long as it was tied up and off the collar.

One of the men had attracted Drill Sergeant Benson's attention. The guy had film star good looks and a hair style not unlike Donny Osmond.

"Who the hell do you think you are, fucking Shirley Temple?" shouted the Drill Sergeant.

Lucy was shocked, she had only heard the F word once before.

"No Drill Sergeant," he answered. The sarcasm in his voice was evident.

"Right then, I want to see all those curly locks off and you looking more like a police officer in training than a pop star waiting to go on stage."

"No Drill Sergeant."

"What the fuck do you mean no Drill Sergeant?"

"I mean I will not be cutting my hair," said the young man with determination in his voice.

"Well sonny Jim, if you want to stay at this college and later join the ranks of the active police officers you will be having that lot off."

"In that case, Drill Sergeant, I won't be joining."

To everyone's amazement the guy left the ranks, picked up his belongings and left. Lucy was stunned. Surely, she thought, he must have known that a regulation haircut was mandatory even at the interview stage.

The remaining officers were given twenty minutes to go to their rooms and put on their uniforms.

***

"Fall in, I said fall in you rabble!" The Drill Sergeant shook his head.

"I do not believe what I'm seeing. Where have you lot been all your lives, smoking pot and dancing naked around trees?"

He walked up and down the shabby line stopping occasionally to look at one of the new officers and shaking his head in exaggerated disbelief.

"My name is Drill Sergeant Benson. That's spelt B.A.S.T.A.R.D. We will lose twenty-five per cent of you lot before this course is done. I will use every method I can, fair and unfair, to trip you up, find you out and reveal the flaws in your character. This is my army issue pace stick," he said holding up a well-worn stick, "and there's a notch in it for everyone I've failed here."

He stood in front of Lucy and looked her up and down. "How the hell did you slip in? I didn't realise that the Police Force was so damned desperate."

"I passed every test that was put in front of me Drill Sergeant," she answered promptly.

"Good, but don't you go expecting any special privileges just because you're a woman."

"I don't Drill Sergeant," she quietly replied.

"Right you lot, while you are under my command you will learn the fundamentals of the parade ground which includes marching. You will have your uniform in order, at all times, stay in step and use your peripheral vision and keep the line dressed. When I give the command 'Attention' you are to bring your heels together sharply in line with your toes pointing out equally forming an angle of forty-five degrees. Rest your body evenly on your heels and balls of both feet. Now keep your legs straight without locking the knees. Like so."

His example was followed; it was shabby.

"What is your name?" Sergeant Benson towered over Clare. She was visibly distressed but before she could answer a redheaded WPC at the back shouted, "Jelly Belly, Drill Sergeant." It was an obvious dig at Clare being slightly overweight and was met with a raft of childish giggles.

"Shut it McCambridge! Speak when you are spoken too and not before."

"Yes, Drill Sergeant," she smirked. "My name is Clare, Drill Sergeant."

"Clare what?"

"Clare Whitfield, Drill Sergeant."

"Well WPC Clare Whitfield, stand upright with an assertive and correct posture. Chin up, chest out, shoulders back and stomach in. Do you understand?"

"Yes, Drill Sergeant."

"Good. Right, now all of you. When I give the command 'Stand at Ease' you are to simultaneously move your left foot only, out shoulder width, while reaching both hands behind your back. Interlock the thumbs and hold then right above your waistline."

The command was followed.

"Good that's better WPC Clare Whitfield."

Drill Sergeant Benson walked up and down the line several times.

"Your training will include both academic and physical classes from Monday through to Thursday. On Friday mornings you will be tested and your results will be posted in the main block on Monday morning. If you fail, then you get to do it again. Let me be clear, if you do not meet the standards of today's modern police force then," he grinned, "you will be weeded out and removed. Only the best pass through my command and this establishment. Do you understand!"

"Yes, Drill Sergeant," they all answered as one.

"I will be personally overseeing your gym and swimming. We do not include this in your training because you will be spending your time doing physical exercise. It is meant to tax your body and prey on your instincts. You will be scored on your ability to undertake specific tasks and activities that will show clearly if you can perform the duties of a police officer. This training is designed to do just one thing – cut out those who can't cut it."

He paused and noted their expressions. "Out there, in the real world, you will have to jump fences at a dead run, sprint down streets and alleys, scramble through gardens, climb chain link, avoid barking dogs, knives and maybe even firearms. You will have to tackle or struggle with violent suspects who may be under the influence of drugs or alcohol."

Drill Sergeant Benson took his place in the centre of the line facing the trainees. "I expect all of you to rise to our daily challenges armed with enthusiasm, excitement and the anticipation of excellence. You need to be fit, clear headed and ready to give your all. Is that clear WPC Clare Whitfield?"

"Yes, Drill Sergeant Benson," replied Clare. Her voice was quavering.

"By the end of this ten week training period you will need to be able to complete a one and a half mile run in eighteen minutes or less. If you fail, you do not move on. There will be pursuit runs. That's sprints from a standing start over one hundred yards and includes a fence climb at the end of the sprint. Your time to complete this is eighty-five seconds or less. There will also be strength tests, which will include bench pressing a percentage of your body weight, twenty sit ups and twenty push ups both to be completed within one minute or quicker. These exercises will be strenuous. When you arrive take time to warm up and stretch. This will relax you and bring your body up to speed. Okay, last but not least there will be, during your final week, a two-mile swim. That is one hundred and twenty-eight lengths of the pool. We've seen more officers fail here than anywhere else so stay sharp and keep focused."

The trainees looked at each other, some smiling, others clearly concerned. Lucy was excited and was trying hard to contain her enthusiasm.

"This training course will be intense, stressful, eye opening but very rewarding. By the time I've finished with you, you'll be a different person. Be proud," he said sternly, "that you have chosen the police force as your career."

Chapter 4

The college had a long L-shaped bar with wooden slats where the trainee officers congregated in the evenings. The barman was called Shaun. He had blonde, wavy hair and piercing blue eyes. Shaun made it his business to introduce himself to everyone who drank at his bar.

Lucy had ordered a whisky with ginger ale. She sipped it cautiously as it was the first time that she'd drank alcohol in a bar.

"Well, look who it is, the fab four," sneered Gwendolyn McCambridge. "I have to say, Clare – Clare Whitfield isn't it? That new hair style really suits you."

"Thank you," answered Clare running her fingers through her hair.

"Yes," Gwendolyn continued, "it makes you look so much thinner. Tell me have you ever had a boyfriend?"

"That's enough," interrupted Lucy. "Go and annoy someone else."

"Really," continued Gwendolyn, "some people have no sense of humour." She motioned Shaun the Barman to fill her glass and left.

"She's quite the Miss that one, for sure," said Shaun. "What's her problem?" asked Karen.

"I'm not sure that she has any problems at all. The word has it that daddy is some big shot at Scotland Yard so she's being fast tracked through here and beyond."

"Well that explains her natural arrogance," concluded Lucy.

"Come here." Shaun motioned them towards him and, with the flat of his hand beside his mouth, he whispered, "She arrived a few days before everyone else and just two nights ago she ordered whisky and cokes like they were going out of fashion. She sank one down after another and began to slur her words and stumble around. I thought it best to ask her to take it easy. I'm not kidding you she bolted upright, grabbed my ear lobe and pulled my head across the bar, knocking off and breaking several of these glasses in the process. Then without a slur and as clear as day she told me, in her posh privileged accent, never to cut her off ever again. She then went on to tell me that I was nothing but an ignorant potato growing, thick Mick. You know, the usual, let's have a go at a Paddy type thing. Anyway a few seconds later she staggered towards the Ladies and then threw up all over the floor. It was nasty, for sure."

"So, what happened next?" asked Clare.

"A couple of the senior female officers carried her back to her room. It was all hushed up. WPC Gwendolyn McCambridge is a feisty young lady and from what I've seen so far, well she's above the laws that govern us. You'd best all watch yourselves."

"That's disgraceful," said Clare.

"Not very lady like at all," offered Laura.

"She's dangerous, so we'd best keep our wits about us," said Lucy with a nervous grin.

"So, do you have any advice for trainees like us?" asked Karen.

"No not really," said Shaun slowly shaking his head. "Only kidding." he laughed. "This is probably the best advice I can give. Teamwork will get you through even if all else fails. Make as many friends as you can, swap notes and share experiences both good and bad. Having friends to share the challenges with will be invaluable, so it will. Be prepared because this place will test your very limits and you will see friends fall away."

"Thank you," said Laura. "Is there anything else?"

"Yes, make sure all your personal shit stays outside the college. This place, and believe me, because I've seen it first hand, will take a lot out of you mentally, so you really shouldn't have anything else to worry about. So, ladies, park up your mum, dad, husband or boyfriend issues. It might sound like a small thing, but it will make all the difference. You really must fully engage in every aspect of your training. Now, with all that said, can I get anyone a drink?"

They all swallowed down their drinks in a single gulp and ordered the same again.

"You must have seen some real sights here Shaun?" said Clare.

"Oh, I have for sure, but I don't want to be telling stories that'll get me into trouble."

"Oh, come on Shaun, just the one. We all promise that it won't go any further."

Shaun smiled, his big blue eyes lighting up. "Okay just the one for tonight."

The girls huddled back around Shaun as he dried a glass, looked around to make sure no one needed serving and began.

"There was a young trainee who came through by the name of Andy. I can't remember his surname now but anyway he was a nice guy. There were times when his voice would change, and a broad London accent would find its way out. This was normally after several pints with whisky chasers. Everyone liked Andy, but he was a real maverick, which didn't always go down well here. It was getting close to the end of the course and Andy had been struggling with the two-mile swim. Well, on this particular night, he let himself go and swallowed down pint after pint of Strongbow Cider and chaser after chaser. When time out was called at 10.30 he went back to his room like everyone else. Only I didn't realise it, but he had nicked a full bottle of Bells Whisky from behind the bar. Then, during the early hours of the morning, he had run from block to block knocking on doors and running away laughing like a mad man. He was found in the morning with his trousers and underwear around his ankles, lying unconscious in a puddle of piss. If that wasn't bad enough, Andy had shit his pants and then used it to write 'Benson is a Bastard' on the canteen wall. Andy never made it. He was ushered out and never seen again".

The girls were in hysterics.

"That is the funniest story I've ever heard," laughed Clare.

"Don't forget now," Shaun reminded them, "Mum's the word okay?"

"Here girls," said Laura, "have you seen that guy over there by the Juke Box? He keeps looking over here at me. Do you think I should go over, or wait for him to pluck up the courage and say hello?"

"I think Laura," said Lucy, "for what it's worth, that he looks like what he probably is, a womaniser."

"What do you mean a womaniser?" said Laura.

"Look I don't know him from Adam and I might be wrong, but to me he looks like the kind of man who needs to control everyone, to him it's all about the power. He uses woman like us as a means to an end. It has nothing to do with the sex act because as far as a man like that is concerned sex is a bonus, but domination is the prize!"

"Wow that's a bit harsh Lucy."

"Yes, I know but you did ask what I thought," Lucy replied.

The guy wore blue, flared denim jeans and a white, open necked shirt with a gold medallion hanging down his very hairy chest. He drew heavily on his cigarette and held up his hand in a gesture of friendliness and beckoned Laura over.

Laura smiled and tossed her long blonde pigtails. "I'm going to put a record on. Any requests?"

"Yeah, what about 'I Can't give you anything (but my love)' by The Stylistics or 'The Hustle' by Van McCoy?" said Clare with a smile.

"More like 'S.O.S' by Abba," said Lucy sarcastically.

Laura shot Lucy a look with half closed eyes and headed away.

"I bet you see a lot of that Shaun," said Karen raising an eyebrow.

"You mean romances or plain old indiscreet liaisons?" he smiled. "Sure, as a barman who's worked all over the UK I've seen it all. It's not unusual for a beautiful woman to use her body to get what she wants. There are officers here who would take what's on offer, but that won't cut the lady any slack come examination time."

"I don't think Laura will be needing any of that kind of help Shaun," said Lucy sternly.

"I'm sure she won't, but Mr Medallion man isn't exactly new to this."

"Hey Shaun," called out Clare who was now feeling a little tipsy, "They'll be calling time out soon. What about one last story? They do so make me laugh."

"Okay Clare, just for you. We had a young man here called Angus. He was Scottish and had moved down south as a child but retained his broad Scottish accent. Angus liked to bet. He would try and bet his classmates at just about everything be it pool, darts, cards or even obscure stuff like what star signs people were. Well a bunch of the lads got him absolutely legless and then bet him £1 that he couldn't hammer his foreskin to the bar."

"Oh my God, you mean his penis?" giggled Clare.

"Well, not his penis just the foreskin," Shaun replied. "Well they handed him a claw hammer and a two inch tack. Angus sighed deeply, puffed out his chest, undid his trousers and placed this enormous penis on the bar. Everyone was in hysterics and egging him on. He downed his whisky and proceeded to nail his foreskin to the bar."

"That is terrible, he must have been in agony," said Lucy. "Why didn't anyone try to stop him?"

"Dunno," Shaun shrugged his shoulders, "but we had to call an ambulance and Angus was taken away. Needless to say, we never saw poor Angus again. Can you see a pattern emerging from these stories?" he asked in a joking way.

Lucy looked over at Laura and Medallion Man. They were jigging around playfully to 'The Bump by Kenny'. She spotted him run his hand across Laura's bottom. Those around the pair were pointing and talking in whispers. Lucy knew that Laura was a big and very capable girl. She didn't doubt that she could look after herself, but she was still concerned for her new friend.

The bell rang, it was 10.30pm, time for everyone to return to their rooms. 'Lights out' was at 11.30pm and anyone caught outside their allotted building or in their room with the lights on after this time would be in big trouble.

Chapter 5

"Today we are going to discuss *Mens rea*," said the tutor. "It is defined as an element of criminal responsibility, a guilty mind, a guilty or wrongful purpose." He stood up from his chair and continued. "It is a fundamental purpose of criminal law that a crime consists of both a mental and physical element. *Mens rea* is a person's awareness of the fact that his or her conduct is criminal and the act itself is the physical element. Most of today's crimes are defined by statutes that usually contain a word or phrase indicating a *Mens rea* requirement. For example: act, knowingly, purposely or recklessly."

The tutor took out some papers and passed them amongst the trainees.

"Now this is your test paper. I shall read it with you and then I want you to discuss this with your friends and colleagues and hand in your conclusions tomorrow morning.

A sweet little old lady named Betty was about to become ninety years old. She decided to celebrate her birthday and invite all her friends for tea and cakes. When she went off to the shops she discovered that the cost of the best cakes were more than she could afford. After a little thought, she looked up and down the aisle, checking that nobody was watching, on seeing that she was alone, she placed several boxes of Gateaux cakes and Fondant Fancies into her bag. She began to leave the shop. This was something that Betty had never done before, and as much as she wanted the cakes as a treat for her friends, she was overwhelmed by guilty feelings, so she removed the cakes from her bag and placed them back on the shelf."

The tutor faced the trainees and pointed his finger towards the class. "Did Betty commit any crime or break any laws?"

Gwendolyn cleared her throat catching the classes attention, "I think Karen wanted to say something quite profound and sensible. But didn't know how." A couple of the class sniggered.

"That's quite enough McCambridge," said the tutor clearing his paperwork.

Lucy looked over at Karen; she was aware that she had been struggling in all the classes and was becoming increasingly distant. As they left the class Lucy asked, "Are you okay Karen?"

"Not really, I'm really struggling with all this law stuff. It just opens up so many questions in my head and I find it hard to draw a conclusion. Then when I do, it's not the same as everyone else's," said Karen making a sad face.

"Tell you what," smiled Lucy, "let's give the bar a miss tonight and I'll come to your room. We can study together and discuss this until you understand it, okay?"

"Do you mind Lucy? I don't want to impose," Karen replied softly.

"Come on Karen, we're friends. I'm more than happy to help. We can make up the lost drinks on Monday when we get our exam results. Sound good?" Lucy winked.

"Sounds great. I really can't fail Lucy. My family need me to do this, and I need to do this for my brother. I just want the family to be happy and proud again."

The class arrived dressed in sports training wear and were met by Drill Sergeant Benson.

"Okay, we are now on week five and half way through the course. Today you will be tested on the pursuit sprint from a standing start. Fall in, move, move, move!"

The class formed a line. Lucy was the first to go. She could see the fence ahead, gritted her teeth and bolted off the start line on Drill Sergeant's command. She knew she had a good pace and one hundred yards would be easy. Slowing down, just a little, she launched into the air and over the fence climb at the end of the sprint.

"Seventy-nine seconds Penfold, you're through," said the Drill Sergeant. "Right, Whitfield you're next."

Lucy watched as Clare ran towards the fence climb. "Come on Clare, you can do it!" she said, punching the air and egging her on. Clare smiled and slowed down at the fence climb. She jumped clumsily reaching for the top, then again, and again, finally collapsing in floods of tears.

"Don't you cry on me Whitfield. That was totally unsatisfactory. Only two more chances Whitfield and then you're out," said the Drill Sergeant.

Clare stood up with her head down, wiping away the tears.

"You have a poor mental attitude. Walk around Whitfield, walk around!" The Drill Sergeant said, but he looked concerned.

"I'm in trouble Lucy. I'm not sure I can make it," sobbed Clare.

"You'll be fine. It's Bensons job to be a bastard. Look, let's give the weekend leave a miss now until the end of the course and just train. It'll help us both. This is a walk in the park compared to that two-mile swim."

"Yeah, thanks Lucy. We'll show that bastard we can do anything that's thrown at us."

"I heard that Whitfield, Penfold. Drop down and give me twenty press ups now!"

"Yes, Drill Sergeant."

Both the girls dropped down and began to do the press ups.

"Get your face down there, I want the tip of your nose touching the ground!"

"Yes, Drill Sergeant."

Chapter 6

It was week nine and a Monday night. Those who had failed were gone and the remaining officers were in the bar celebrating.

"I wonder what's happened to Karen? She left on Friday and didn't turn up this morning. I know she's been struggling but she's soldiered on," said Lucy taking a sip from her whisky and ginger ale.

"I don't know, but people are dropping like flies. I can't believe I'm still here. I really owe you," smiled Clare patting Lucy on the arm. "If we hadn't trained together over the weekends I would never have made it through physical."

"We're not out the woods yet, we still have that two-mile swim remember?" said Lucy.

"I'm doing everything you said Lucy, tackling the challenge in bite size chunks. I did over one hundred and fifty lengths on Sunday. By the end of the course I'm sure I'll be ready," grinned Clare.

"Good for you" replied Lucy "You can get me the next drink then," both girls laughed.

The juke box played 'I Wanna Dance Wit Choo by Disco Tex & The Sex-o-Lettes'. Groups of trainees got up and began dancing. Lucy spotted Laura laughing out loud and jigging around suggestively with Medallion Man.

"Hi Lucy, I'm Ben," said a voice from behind her. Lucy turned to see a short, dark haired guy with a large bulbous nose. She recognised him as a friend of Medallion Man.

"Oh hi," she said as a look of puzzlement passed briefly across her face.

"I was wondering," said Ben. "Wondering what?" quizzed Lucy.

"Well there's this new movie about this killer shark that goes around killing everyone. It's called Jaws," he spluttered nervously, "and I've heard lots of great reviews about it. It's on in the town and wondered if you'd come and see it with me on Saturday."

Lucy shook her head. "I'm sorry Ben but I have commitments at the weekend."

"It's okay Lucy, I can train on my own if you want to go Saturday," shrugged Clare.

"No," Lucy shot her a stern look, "we'll do the training as planned."

She turned and smiled at Ben. "Listen Ben, I'm sure that you're a nice guy but," she paused briefly, "I am not looking for a boyfriend, a relationship or anything that could distract me getting through this course. I'm sure that you understand."

"Yeah sure, okay. It's just that you seem like a person who would be great company."

Medallion Man approached the bar and beckoned Shaun over snapping his fingers. "Shaun mate, I'd like a Pernod and black and a pint of lager please."

Shaun nodded.

"Looks like your lot have been blowing the fuck out of London again," Medallion Man said with a smile.

"My lot?" Shaun nodded wearily.

"Yeah, your lot, the bloody IRA," replied Medallion Man.

"Not my lot," replied Shaun in an aggravated tone. "If they were, you lot would all be dead by now."

"Good point Shaun, not bad for a Mick," said Medallion Man as he turned and smiled at Lucy.

"You and Laura seem to be getting along well," said Lucy in a sarcastic tone.

"Yeah, you know how it is," replied Medallion Man.

"No, I don't know how it is. Tell me, what did you think when you first saw Laura? How did you feel, was it love at first sight?" Lucy asked with even more sarcasm in her voice.

"Not quite," he smirked. "I took one look at her beautiful long blonde pigtails and thought, I've hit the jackpot here, it's a blow job with handlebars." He picked up the drinks, winked and walked away.

"I'm sorry about that," said Ben. I know he can come across as an arrogant twat sometimes, but he really is a good guy at heart."

"Oh, I'm sorry. Are you still here?" said Lucy angrily. "No, just going. If you change your mind..."

Lucy interrupted him. "I won't." "Another drink ladies?" asked Shaun.

"Yeah why not, we're celebrating. Only two weeks to go," said Clare trying to calm the atmosphere. "People like Medallion Man really get on my wick. They're so bloody full of themselves with about as much depth as a Rizla roll up paper."

"Would you like to hear another story?" asked Shaun. "Sure, fire away," smiled Clare enthusiastically.

"Well, a few years back we had this guy called Robert here. He must have been part of the country set, if you know what I mean, because he turned up with his own shotgun. At weekends he would go to the local farms and shoot wildlife, without asking permission from the land owners. On one occasion he was out shooting when an agitated farmer shouted at him from a distance. Now Robert knew that what he was doing was actually poaching, so he dropped the shotgun and ran. Fortunately it was dark and the farmer probably didn't get a clear view of him, but when Robert got back here he began worrying and decided on a course of action."

"What, what did he do?" questioned Clare enthusiastically with a broad smile.

"Robert got out his police uniform, put it on and then walked over to the farmer's house. He was invited in and Robert informed the farmer that the police had a poacher in custody and that he was calling to collect the shotgun as evidence. The farmer laughed and apparently said 'I have never reported the incident to the Police, so please enlighten me as to how you REALLY know about it.' Robert began to fluster, saying that they had a confession and if he could just have the shotgun he'd be on his way. Well this farmer was no fool. He sensed that something just didn't add up, so he told Robert that he would get his coat and come down to the station. He wanted to see the poacher and talk to Robert's superior officer. Now Robert was panicking. This was going to another level, so, seeing no other way out, he admitted that it was him that was out shooting on the farmer's land. He apologised and stated that he didn't mean any harm and that if he could just have his shotgun back he'd be on his way.

"So, did the farmer give Robert the shotgun?"

"Not a chance, the wily old farmer got his coat and drove down to the police station. Robert was charged, drummed out and never seen again."

"Rightly so," said Lucy still angry about Medallion Man's remarks.

Somebody put on 'Hold Me Close by David Essex' on the juke box and everyone in the bar began singing along. Lucy loosened up, knocked back her drink, smiled and joined in.

Gwendolyn ran through the bar, bent down and pulled the juke box's electric plug out of the wall. "Listen up people!" she said excitedly. "Hot off the press, people!" she exclaimed. "Laura loose elastic has just been caught by the night Patrol Sergeants, having it off with some guy behind the bike shed and they have both been sent to the Commandant's Office!" Gwendolyn was beaming with delight.

Lucy couldn't believe what she'd heard. She was embarrassed that Gwendolyn had made this information a public announcement, but could not understand how Laura could find herself in that situation. Lucy turned to Shaun on her way out. "Looks like you have another story to tell now."

***

Later that evening after lights out at 11.30pm Lucy snuck out of her room and across the landing, down the stairs into the all- girls dormitory. She got down on all fours, scrambled across the floor in the dark until she found Laura's bed.

"Laura, Laura are you awake?" she whispered. "Yes, what are you doing here?"

"I was worried about you, I wanted to see if you were okay." "I'm okay, I suppose. All things considered."

"What were you thinking about Laura? You must be mad."

"I know what it looks like Lucy but it all just kind of happened. It was just love, heat and passion."

"Really?"

"Yes, really Lucy. I really like him," Laura said dreamily. "It's like, well you've heard that the eyes are like the window to the soul. Well that was it for me. I just looked into his eyes and they just captivated me. I fell head over heels for him. He really does have the most amazing qualities. He's funny, attentive and," she paused with a smile, "he knows just how to treat a lady if you know what I mean. Lucy I've messed around with guys and never and I mean never did I climax unless I did it myself. He made me feel, well, just wow!"

"That all sounds well and good Laura, but what happens now?"

"I don't know. I have to see Benson in the morning." "Bloody hell Laura, I don't want to lose you."

"Don't worry about me Lucy. Everything will be alright. You'd better get yourself back to your room or we'll both be getting drummed out."

"Okay, I'll see you in the morning."

"Goodnight Lucy"

"Goodnight Laura."

Chapter 7

Lucy knocked on Drill Sergeant Benson's office door.

"Come in!"

Lucy entered the small office. She spotted several pictures of the Sergeant receiving medals and noticed scores of trophies on the back shelf.

"Take a seat Penfold."

"Drill Sergeant, I was hoping to talk with you about what happened last night."

"I half expected you to come in and try to fight a case Penfold."

"It's just that Laura is a good officer and a good friend who made a stupid mistake."

"Penfold, she's gone."

"What, you mean drummed out?"

"No Penfold. Like you, I saw a good trainee who made a mistake. A bloody king size stupid mistake but, I didn't feel it warranted her permanent removal. Your friend left here in the early hours of this morning. She will complete her training in Ashford, Kent."

"Thank you, Drill Sergeant," Lucy smiled with relief. Drill Sergeant Benson leant across the table.

"I do have some bad news Penfold."

"What Sir?"

"WPC Karen White took her life on Saturday."

Lucy's heart sank, tears began to fill her eyes and her voice trembled. "Oh no! What happened?"

"I'm sorry Penfold but I think your friend may have had some unresolved issues. She took her father's hunting rifle and killed herself."

Lucy couldn't help herself, tears began to flood from her eyes uncontrollably. She was heartbroken. She had lost Laura and now Karen, her good friend and fellow officer, was dead.

"I'm going to leave now Penfold. Take a few minutes to sort yourself out and then join us on the parade ground."

"Yes, I will. Thank you, Drill Sergeant."

***

Lucy joined her class. As she sat down, the door flew open and a man wearing a black balaclava, with holes cut out for his eyes and mouth, ran in brandishing a sawn-off shotgun.

"On the floor!" he shouted at the tutor. "Get on the fucking floor. You lot stay where you are, don't move or I'll blow your fucking heads off!"

The class looked at each, unsure of what was happening. Nobody moved.

The gun man held out a black bag, ordered the tutor to get on his knees and put the barrel to his head. "Take off your watch, get your wallet and place them in this bag. Hurry up you piece of shit!" The gun man lifted his leg and kicked the tutor to the ground.

"Right, I'm leaving now but my associate is outside so if any of you move within the next five minutes he'll blow you away. Understand?"

There was no answer.

The gun man placed the barrel at Clare's head. "I said do you understand?"

"Yes," the class replied as one.

He kicked the tutor again and backed out the door pointing the gun.

There was unrest and a commotion. The tutor stood up. "Right class, that was today's exercise. As witnesses to the crime I want you all to write a statement for discussion this afternoon."

Chapter 8

The training course was almost complete. Lucy had been reflecting on her experiences at Cwmbran. Her friend Laura had been moved to Ashford Kent, Karen had sadly taken her life, but Clare had come along in leaps and bounds. Starting slightly overweight she had struggled with the physical aspects of the training but excelled in all else. Together they had trained, the weight fell off Clare but more importantly her mental attitude changed. She became strong, focused and determined. Even when Gwendolyn joked about Karen's suicide by passing a comment that Karen had gone to the college library first to get a book on suicide but they wouldn't let her have it for fear she wouldn't return it, they stayed strong, let it pass and kept focused on the finishing line.

Lucy was amongst the first to do the two-mile swim and completed it within ninety minutes, just a few minutes off the college record. Clare followed remembering all their training. Understanding that despite being in water it was still physical exercise and she would sweat, she drank and kept her body hydrated and ate forty-five minutes before starting, ensuring her body would have sufficient energy to complete the task.

Cheered on by her team mates Clare completed the challenge in one hundred and one minutes.

When Lucy saw Gwendolyn swim easily through the water on her way to completing the task she felt an overwhelming need to do something, tip the balance of natural justice. Noticing that no one was paying attention she waited patiently until the closing laps and then slipped into the pool without being seen. Lucy took a deep breath and swam out under Gwendolyn, grabbed her leg hard and pulled her under the water with a sharp tug. It had gone unnoticed. Gwendolyn was under water wriggling and kicking but almost out of energy after one hundred and fifty laps. Lucy let go, slipped out the pool quickly and was back amongst her friends. Gwendolyn resurfaced spluttering and coughing. She struggled to the side of the pool choking and trying desperately to empty her lungs from pool water.

Drill Sergeant Benson leant down and lifted her clean out the pool. "That's a failure WPC MCCambridge, only two more chances and you're out!"

Lucy smiled to herself whilst feigning concern.

***

It was the final day and each of the remaining trainees were being called into Drill Sergeant Benson's office.

"Congratulations WPC Penfold. I'm pleased to inform you you've passed the training. Law enforcement is a unique profession. Providing you win trust, demonstrate loyalty and give your all to the job you will be part of the so-called brotherhood of the thin blue line. Working as a police officer offers a sense of belonging and family that you simply will not find in other careers. When the chips are down you can be sure your fellow officers will be there for you.

There will be no greater feeling than when you've done something to make someone else's life just a little bit better. Even something simple like showing compassion and empathy at a traffic accident or helping to see that justice is done for the victims of crime. Most of us took the job because we wanted to help others.

Officers rarely think about it, but they save lives every day. Sometimes, it'll make the news when an officer races into a burning building to save a child or when they put themselves in danger to protect the innocent and defenceless. There are countless other times your work will go unnoticed, but through your actions, maybe a person will change their driving habits after a few speeding endorsements on their driving licence or a drunk driver will be banned. Maybe, just maybe a would-be robber could change their mind because a patrol car passed by.

In these modern times it is said that everyone hates the police until they need them. The fact is police officers still enjoy a measure of respect within the community and are often looked at as leaders and examples to be followed.

The bottom line, WPC Penfold, is this: being a police officer is both fun and rewarding. It's not just another nine to five job. It becomes part of who and what you are. There are not too many professions that can really get into your blood like law enforcement can.

Throughout this course you've demonstrated the ability to think before you speak. I've witnessed you think long and hard before giving an answer, especially on important questions. You rarely conform for the sake of fitting in and you're not afraid to be wrong. I like the way you trust your gut feelings and your ability to solve problems.

Now with all this said WPC Penfold you're probably feeling like Billy the Bollocks but believe me when I tell you that you have so much more to learn."

"Thank you, Drill Sergeant Benson. I'll never forget you."

"No WPC Penfold you won't." Drill Sergeant Benson smiled for the first time, and shook her hand. "Now get out of here!"

***

Lucy and Clare crossed the parade ground towards the taxi. Lucy spotted Gwendolyn out of the corner of her eye.

"Wait a minute Clare, I just want to have a few words with our friend." She left her case and raced back across the stained concrete. "Gwendolyn, have you got a minute?" asked Lucy.

Gwendolyn looked at her watch and hissed, "Okay but it needs to be quick."

"I would like to say that despite our many differences and after ten weeks training together I wish you all the best for the future." She paused for a few seconds, "But that's not the case. You are the most repugnant person I have ever met in my life. You have, daily, demonstrated every abhorrent, odious and deplorable characteristic possible. You are loathsome and a judicious imbecile. You're laudably culpable, boorish, self-centred and tactless. You are foolish, witless, dull and in my view unworthy of that proud uniform. Goodbye Gwendolyn McCambridge," Lucy nodded and spun away.

Chapter 9

It was close to Christmas 1975. Hot Chocolate dominated the radio with 'You Sexy Thing', and Lucy, Clare and Laura had settled at Exeter Police Station.

Inspector Jessica Jones had called them all together.

"There's a children's home for wayward girls on Harvester Road. It is not unusual for the girls to wander off or run away. Normally to no further than the café in the High Street, although some have been known to go on shoplifting sprees. I would like the three of you to go on foot patrol, wearing your police capes, and take a good look around."

"Are we looking for anyone, in particular, Ma'am,?" asked Lucy.

"No, but I do want you to split up. Don't take this as an opportunity to go for a gossip. I want you ladies to find out what's going on, okay?"

"Yes Ma'am," replied Lucy.

Once outside, Lucy and Laura walked towards the High Street. It was bitterly cold, and they hadn't seen anything that looked suspicious. Lucy suggested a cup of piping hot tea to keep the cold out. Within just a few minutes Clare arrived.

"We are being so naughty," laughed Laura.

"Well that's not unusual for you is it Laura. I mean if it wasn't loose elastic as your middle name then it most certainly would be naughty," grinned Clare cheekily.

"What do you mean by loose elastic?" demanded Laura half smiling.

"Oh, come on Laura. There's no denying it. Those knickers of yours see more action than a fireman's pole on Bonfire night," joked Lucy.

"Well I never!" gasped Laura, "Now that is very definitely not true."

"There is always someone, somewhere trying to get into the contents of your knickers Laura, and there's no denying it," said Clare smiling bravely.

Laura smiled and gave out a short laugh. "Well what can I say ladies? When you have it," rubbing her hands over her shapely body, "it's just in demand!"

"There you go... naughty just like I said," smirked Clare taking a sip from her tea.

"Tell you what," said Lucy, "when we're done here, why don't we take a walk around the shops? They're warm, we can keep an eye out for wayward girls on the run, plus," she paused, "we can do a bit of shopping."

"Good idea," said Clare excitedly.

Later that afternoon, just after 6pm, the girls returned to the nick.

"Quick, cross your arms and hide your shopping under your capes," said Lucy mischievously.

As they entered the station, Inspector Jessica Jones was waiting.

"Right you lot, in here!"

They were led through to her office. She pointed at Clare. "What have you got under your cape girl?"

Clare's chin started to wobble, her eyes began to redden. She fumbled with her fingers. "I'm sorry, " Clare started to blub, "it was just a few things."

"Get out of my sight, I cannot bear weak women!" the Inspector said impatiently.

Lucy and Laura looked at each other and hunched their shoulders. Although Lucy was scared stiff, terrified, in fact, she would not let it show.

"You girl, what have you got?" The Inspector scowled and pointed at Laura.

"Err nothing Mum. I didn't buy anything", replied Laura her voice uptight.

"Call me Ma'am not bloody Mum when you address me! Get out of here and don't let me see you again today!"

Lucy took a deep breath, she was anxious but still refused to let it show.

"You!", bellowed Inspector Jessica Jones who was clearly agitated,

"What have you got?"

Lucy smiled broadly. "Well Ma'am, I popped into the shops and brought a few things for my family for Christmas." Lucy presented a shopping bag from under her cape, and placed it onto the Inspector's desk.

"This is a white shirt for my dad. He's a long distance lorry driver and I know he would like it. Marks and Spencer's had a special sale and I just had to get it. Here is a bottle of Charlie." Lucy sprayed a little. "Now don't you think that's just divine? I got this for my mum. She hardly ever shops for perfume and with Christmas coming I thought, well, I thought it would be a nice present."

"You're not scared of me are you?" Inspector Jones said. It was more of a statement than a question.

Lucy gave a discreet grin and raised an eyebrow in mock surprise.

"Go on," she said with wry smile, "on your way."

"Yes Ma'am," Lucy replied respectfully.

"Wait one minute." The Inspector reached into her desk and handed Lucy a scrap of note paper.

"I want you to go to this address and see the woman written down here. Her boyfriend has a history of physical abuse, real nasty piece of work and she's just let him back into the house. I want you to then tell HIM that Inspector Jones said pack your bags because you're out! Can you do that Sprog?"

Lucy passed a brief look of puzzlement. The inspector had just called her Sprog. A nickname, she smiled, it was a term of endearment. I think she likes me, Lucy thought to herself.

"Yes Ma'am. I'll do that right away."

***

Lucy delivered the message and the recipient didn't argue. He lowered his head and confirmed that he would be gone in the morning.

On the way back to the nick Lucy was radioed and asked to stop to attend a burglar alarm report at The Gentleman's Club in Tower Square. Lucy parked up outside the club's building, noticed that it was a car alarm on a brown Jaguar XJ6, straightened her uniform and walked inside. There were several older men standing around the bar. They wore a variety of country style checked jackets.

"Excuse me," she beckoned the barman. "I'm here about the alarm."

"What the fucking hell is a woman doing in here?" shouted an elderly man with a grey moustache and thick lensed glasses.

"I'm sorry sir, I'm here about the car alarm outside," Lucy explained.

"Listen here young lady, I don't give a fucking toss about car alarms. You are a member of the female sex and this is a gentleman's club, which means men only, so fuck off!"

"Please sir, let me just do my job and then I'll be on my way," said Lucy.

The older man sucked on his teeth noisily and pulled the barman angrily towards him. "This is a men only club, get that fucking poor excuse of a woman out of here now!"

"Yes, Mr Barnston, I'm sorry Mr Barnston," said the barman apologetically. "Please, can you leave officer. This a gentleman's only club and the members take that very seriously."

"Yes, we damn well do,' Mr Barnston shouted, gesturing furiously towards the door. "Go on fuck off, you cunt!"

Lucy turned to leave, stopped and walked back. She had never been called the C word before and she told herself, they don't pay me enough to be called that.

"You, Mr Barnston, be quiet and drink your beer. If you continue to behave in this way your barman will lose his licence," warned Lucy with her eyes firmly fixed on him.

"You, young lady are a good for nothing cunt. You have no rights to enter a gentleman's establishment. This bar and its members are fucking sacred!" hissed Mr Barnston.

Lucy put her flat palm up indicating that was enough, and walked away.

"Are you reporting us then?'" asked the barman.

"Yes," replied Lucy firmly. "Your licence needs reviewing."

***

Three nights later Lucy was called to the same club. Mr Barnston was standing over his brown Jaguar XJ6.

"Look at this!" he bellowed, pointing at the smashed windscreen.

"You don't recognise me do you sir?" Lucy revealed a smirk that clearly regarded him with contempt.

"Look at my Jaguar, all smashed up by bloody yobbos. What I want to know officer, is what are you going to do about it?"

"You really don't recognise me do you sir?"

"I don't give a flying fuck who you are. I want these vandals hunted down and whipped within an inch of their lives!"

"Really sir?" Lucy looked him up and down. He was unsteady on his feet and reeked of alcohol.

"Yes, fucking really. So, for the last fucking time, what are you going to do about it?"

"For you, Mr Barnston," she leaned forward and hissed, "nothing sir. Goodnight."

Lucy got back into the police car and drove back to the station. On her return she repeated the whole story to the Sergeant. With a tone in his voice that was calm and assured he told Lucy that she had neglected her duties. Lucy lowered her head and acknowledged him. The Sergeant leaned forward and whispered "Lucy, don't ever change." He winked and motioned her on her way, having assured her he would send someone else to deal with the horrible Mr Barnston.

Chapter 10

Lucy had been assigned to the 'knitting circle' to gain more policing experience. The knitting circle was a term used to describe the policewomen's department, and consisted of nine woman police officers including two Sergeants. It was in this department that family data was collated and stored. Members of the knitting circle could advise their colleagues about a potential suspect. They would know who they were married to, their family, children, friends, associates and suspected criminal involvement. It was a rich source of information. If a detective suspected a person or persons of a crime they could first stop and ask members of the knitting circle if there was any information on his family. From their wealth of solid historical data, they could join the dots and confirm friendships, grievances and crime preferences.

Sergeant Pauline Pearson had taken a shine to Lucy. She could see that she learned, adapted and thrived quickly. The two became friendly, chatting over coffee and lunched together most days. Eventually Pauline invited Lucy to her home for dinner with, as she put it, 'her other half'.

"Come in Lucy. Oh that's nice, thank you, " she smiled, taking a bottle of wine from her. "You obviously found us okay?"

"Hi Pauline, yeah it was easy with your instructions." "Come in, come in."

Lucy entered the room and was shown to a brown leather Chesterfield chair.

"Let me get you a glass of wine," said Pauline smiling brightly as she left the room.

"Thank you."

Pauline returned with two glasses of Chardonnay and another woman with long blond hair and a slim figure. The smell of her perfume entered the room." Lucy, I'd like you to meet my girlfriend Gina."

Lucy stood and shook her hand.

"I think you suspected that I was gay, didn't you?"

Lucy giggled shyly. Pauline had an uncanny way of cutting straight through to the point and hitting the nail right on the head.

"I did think that maybe you were. Not that it bothers me. What I mean is that it is your business," said Lucy.

"I know that, which is why I was comfortable inviting you here tonight to share with you a little more of me and not just the Sergeant who runs the knitting circle."

"It's nice to meet you," said Gina nervously. "Pauline has spoken about you often. I'm just about to serve dinner, I hope you like chicken, come on through to the dining room."

***

The friends enjoyed dinner and several glasses of wine. All the initial tensions and concerns quickly disappeared.

"I didn't always know I was a gay," Pauline began to explain. "In fact, believe it or not I was married to a man for almost six years. This wasn't a case of my denying my sexuality. I had never had any desire to be with a woman and certainly never questioned who I wanted to be sexually intimate with. I had always gone out with men, and yet there I was falling in love with Gina after we met at a pub after work one night."

"Wow, so what did you do?" quizzed Lucy.

"I did what I always do when I'm baffled, confused or scared. I popped off to the library and did my research. I started reading everything I could get my hands on about lesbianism and bisexuality. I wanted to cover all aspects because at first I just wasn't sure."

Gina reached across the table, squeezed Pauline's hand and smiled.

"Then one night, about four months into my growing attraction to Gina, I had sex with my husband Ben. This was not the norm. In fact, sex had become a rare occurrence since I was constantly thinking about Gina," she chuckled. "I began realising more and more what actually turned me on, got me excited and what I and many other women needed; the soft, tender loving touch of a woman."

Lucy took a long sip from her wine glass and leaned forward almost motioning Pauline to continue.

"While I was having sex with Ben, I was painfully aware of the roughness of his hands, the coarseness of his unshaven face, the angular sharpness of his body and his penis," she shook her head in disgust. "I just had no interest, at all. It really was kind of amazing how much I did not want him or any man anywhere near me. Don't get me wrong, I had hours of quizzing myself, questioning my feelings and feeling so desperately sorry for my husband for not being Gina. Then I thought about something Gina had said when we met again in the pub after work one Friday. She had a friend with her, who was also gay. At one point her friend rested her head on Gina's shoulder and I could feel myself become very jealous. Gina said that once she got to know a person, really know a person then she would love them. Lucy, I immediately replayed that moment in my mind. I wanted to cry. Later that night, the tears came, fast, hot and bitter. They surprised me and made me feel pretty damn low and sad."

"I'm so sorry," offered Lucy.

Pauline paused, laughed a little and then kissed Gina on the cheek and continued. "I was crying because I was falling head over heels deeply in love with Gina. I was getting to know her; the real person and I was falling in love. I ached for her and I wanted Gina to know me and love me too. The weight of that was just so heavy. I was married. Gina was with someone. I loved her. Ben loved me. It was horrible, heart breaking. During the entire time we spent together at the pub or at lunch it took everything in me not to tell Gina that I was falling in love with her. I fought and struggled not to reach out and connect with her in any way. I had to suppress just how excited and happy I was to see her, hear about what she was doing, saying or thinking. I fought desperately not to tell her thirty times a day just how beautiful I thought she was."

Pauline emptied the contents of her glass and Gina left the room to refill it.

"I never did tell Gina how I truly felt. I did leave my marriage though. I swore to my husband that there wasn't another man. I did tell him of my growing interest in Gina but that I wasn't gay. He was probably as confused as I was. He told me that he loved me and wanted children and to do all the things a family did. Something just told me that I had to make changes and the stark truth was that I needed to leave. It was one of the hardest things I've ever done in my life. I was leaving a comfortable home and the cosy life time of heteronormativity, I was leaving all that behind and entering a world where woman love other woman. This was a new, unknown territory for me. I was terrified Lucy and yet I had never felt so free in my entire life. Just a few weeks later Gina and I got together. This is a serious relationship, we're committed to each other. She is the woman that I love and adore. In truth it did take some years before my brain accepted that I was a lesbian. Initially I considered myself bisexual having only been out with men my entire life, and even marrying one. I can now say Lucy, without any doubt that I am a lesbian and no one could have more surprised than me."

'That's an amazing story Pauline. I'm so pleased for you and Gina."

"Life is too short to be unhappy Lucy. We don't go shouting from the roof tops that we're gay. It's just who and what we are and to a few special people, who we trust and like, we share the true us."

'Thank you, thank you for trusting me," Lucy nodded.

"So, what about you Lucy Penfold? Despite all the attention at the nick you've never gone out with anyone or been romantically involved?"

"This is difficult, I think that I'm attracted to women too. I'm just not sure."

"Hey," said Gina, "sexual orientation is not a binary. It exists along a spectrum. Because of this identifying your sexual preference and truly accepting your sexual orientation can be a long, complex and emotional journey. Pauline's is a great example," she smiled reassuringly. "Embarking on this process may leave you feeling overwhelmed. I believe that you must remain honest and open with yourself. Trust your instincts Lucy, listen to your body and acknowledge your true feelings and tendencies and then accept what you discover about yourself throughout the process."

'Wow that's deep," Lucy said looking slightly overwhelmed.

"Gina is right," confirmed Pauline. "The decision to explore your sexual orientation should be a personal choice. Questioning your sexuality is a process you will need to complete and that's not because friends or friends of friends say that you're a lesbian. Try to devote some time for self-reflection. Maybe even keep a private diary. It may allow you an outlet for self-exploration and discovery."

"Absolutely," Gina beamed taking a large sip from her wine glass. "Sexually experimenting with members of the same sex is healthy, normal and doesn't mean that you're a lesbian. That said if you find you have frequent or consistent desires to be with a woman instead of men, that may indicate that you are a lesbian."

"You have to ask yourself," interrupted Pauline, "do you check out woman, do you notice a woman's smile, quirks and features? Does your heart race and stomach flutter when you see an attractive woman?"

"Or," asked Gina, "are you sexually aroused by woman or maybe you're daydreaming about a specific woman?"

"I haven't done anything really," Lucy said, "I may have flirted a little with a woman, but she was married and didn't notice or just wasn't interested. As for men, well I have never truly been attracted to any. I had and have some great male friends but have never had a desire, at all, to have sex with any of them."

"I think most of us," said Pauline, topping up all their glasses, "try to avoid or overcompensate for our sexual desires. That's natural.

From personal experience I'd say it's normal to feel scared and maybe a little overwhelmed by it all. The way I moved forward was to allow myself to be vulnerable and honest with myself. I think that was the first step to acknowledging who I am. What I have learnt is that being a lesbian is completely normal. That doesn't mean I have to flaunt it, but living my life the way I was meant to is important. So that journey towards self-acceptance is acknowledging that you are a lesbian. It's a small step in the right direction and the more you become comfortable with your sexual orientation the more you will realise that your sexuality does not define you as an individual."

"Lucy," said Gina boldly, "we live our lives unapologetically. We have to rid ourselves of any guilt or shame. Take a deep breath Lucy and put a smile on your face and tell yourself daily that you are valuable, loved and entitled to lead an authentic life that makes you happy."

"At what point do I come out?" Lucy asked.

"At the moment Lucy, you're not even sure if you are. If, and when you're ready for that, prepare yourself for an emotional, antagonising decision with potential consequences. Before coming out to family, friends and work colleagues, determine whether first it safe to do so. You can talk with Gina or me at any time in the strictest of confidence. It's good to remember that although society portrays a stereotypical lesbian, our community is made up with a diverse from a multitude of backgrounds. In the fullness of time you'll find where you fit."

"What Pauline is saying," said Gina raising her glass, "is that you don't have to settle for a woman who wears jeans, Doctor Martin boots, with a short back and sides haircut."

"This is a lot to take in and I'm really grateful for your advice, but let's say I wanted to go out and meet someone at a party or even in a pub that I like, and then maybe even embark on a relationship. What is the best way to find out if she's a lesbian or even attracted to girls?" asked Lucy raising her eyes quizzically.

"There are no hard and fast rules Lucy and there's certainly no books available at the library to answer those questions. Probably the best way is to find the right moment and just ask her right out. Are you attracted to women? If you receive a back hander then that's a no," chuckled Pauline.

"Yes," chimed in Gina, "if you look on the brighter side she may just say yes and be totally delighted that you asked."

"I probably shouldn't say this, but tomboy styles can be a real giveaway, but that said we know lesbians who dress red hot and have guys swooning, so it's like Pauline said, there are no fast and hard rules."

"What about a woman's mannerisms?" asked Lucy rubbing her chin.

"Well there is the 'I'm a lezzer and proud' sitting position." said Gina, laughing.

"The what?" Lucy started laughing too.

"The 'I'm a lezzer and proud' sitting position is when a girl may spread her legs a little more than necessary when sitting, almost as if she has a bulge between her legs. That and maybe if she walks like a man, you know shoulders hunched forward as if trying to hide her breasts with legs set apart with a slight almost bouncing pace as if the shoes are somehow cushioned. Those can be helpful but there's no escaping the loyal practitioner of the flirtatious dyke smile. It is a fusion of sustained eye contact, tilted head and restrained smile. Don't worry Lucy you will understand it if, and when that happens. I suppose you could count the excess lip licking in-between conversations, touchy hands, sitting slightly too near, frequent nose touching. Oh my gosh the list can go on and on."

"A sure-fire sign is short finger nails."

"Yeah, short fingers nails that's a good one Pauline. So, if you're eying up a girl with half inch-long nails then she most definitely isn't a lesbian."

"Oh, my God, too much information!" gasped Lucy laughingly. "I suppose, having listened to all that, what I really need to do is trust my gut instinct."

"Spot on Lucy, always trust your instincts."

Gina left the table and brought back a huge slice of black forest gateau and a new bottle of wine under her arm. "Don't worry we can call you a taxi to get back to your quarters Lucy. It's been fun having you here and don't worry your secrets are as safe as ours are with you." smiled Pauline.

***

Later back in her quarters Lucy laid back on her bed. She felt slightly drunk having consumed the best part of a bottle of Chardonnay. She reflected on the conversations and was still surprised how easily the words had left her mouth even though she had never quite acknowledged them to herself. Lucy felt at peace as if a new chapter in her life was opening.

Chapter 11

"Sprog, I'm going to interview a rape victim and I'd like you to attend. Rape and sexual assaults are horrendous crimes that devastate victims and their families," said Inspector Jessica Jones lighting a cigarette and inhaling deeply.

"Thank you," Lucy replied smiling at the opportunity to gain further policing experience.

"I'd like you to stay quiet and observe," she said raising an eyebrow. "It is almost impossible to analyse the number of rapes and sexual assaults that happen each year because they simply do not get reported."

"Why wouldn't victims come forward?" asked Lucy anxious to understand.

"I don't believe that there's any one reason. I suspect there's feelings of guilt, embarrassment, the fear of not being believed and of course a mistrust of our own justice system. That is why it is essential that officers who are responsible for investigating these crimes play a pivotal role in assuaging victims fears and uncertainties about the justice system. Do you understand?"

"Yes Inspector," Lucy nodded.

"There is the clear issue of consent. The general definition of rape is the penetration of the sexual organ, mouth or anus of one person by another without consent. Now, this can also include sexual relations with a person below a specific age, such as a minor under the age of sixteen. The law also protects people who are mentally deficient and incapable of giving consent. Consent is a leading issue with sex crimes because children cannot consent, intellectually and developmentally disabled people cannot consent, and an intoxicated person cannot consent."

"Okay, I understand," said Lucy, sitting forward.

"The first responding officer generally conducts an initial interview to obtain a description of the offender, the nature of the injuries sustained by the victim and the location of the crime scene. It is imperative Lucy, that during the initial phases of a sex crime investigation you ensure the victim receives proper medical care. In addition, it's beneficial for the victim to consent to a sexual assault examination. The victim's body contains valuable evidence that must be identified, preserved, collected and analysed. In essence the victim is a walking crime scene. During the sexual assault examination, the doctor will document any bruising, abrasions or other injuries on the victim as well as any trauma to the vaginal, penal or anal region. The doctor will collect evidence from the victim that will include semen, hairs, vaginal fluid, blood and trace evidence. So, to summarise, the primary role of the investigating officers are the physical and emotional well being of the victim, the preservation of evidence and the apprehension of the suspect."

She stopped and took another long draw on her cigarette and a sip from her coffee.

"Investigating sexual orientated crimes is challenging for officers because it requires conducting an in-depth interview with the victim without causing further emotional harm. The interview is a vital part of the investigation and must be managed with the utmost of care. It is necessary for the investigator to create a desirable atmosphere to ensure a successful interview. You must remember that some victims of sexual assault and rape are traumatised and feel as though they have lost control over their lives. So, to conduct a successful interview with the rape victim the officer must step out of their traditional role of simply obtaining the facts from a victim, do you understand?"

"Yes, I understand," nodded Lucy seriously.

"So, even before you start interviewing the victim, the officer must build a rapport with the victim, demonstrate empathy and validate her credibility. You must provide the victim with the opportunity to make small choices and let them feel some resemblance of control."

"How do you mean?" asked Lucy.

"Well, ask the victim if she wants someone present with her during the interview and allow her to select the interview location. That said it must be private and free from distractions."

"Okay, I understand."

"Do you know what an open-ended question is?"

"Sure. How, why, when, where and what."

"Good. Smart girl," she smiled raising her eyebrow in a friendly fashion.

"The officer should always open the interview with an open-ended question like, 'what happened today?'. The key objective is to allow the victim to tell their entire story without interruption. Then to add detail or clarify discrepancies the officer may ask the victim more specific questions once she has completed her narrative."

The inspector handed Lucy a notebook and pen.

"You might like to make a note of these. Now, the investigating officer must ensure that the victim provides these essential parts of the interview okay?"

Lucy opened the book and looked up towards her mentor hungry for knowledge.

"You have to understand the victim's behaviour prior to the assault, so question where the victim first came in to contact with the suspect, ask was alcohol a factor or was the rape facilitated by drugs and was the victim alone or with friends who could be potential witnesses. You then need to understand the victim's behaviour during the crime. Ask if there was shoving, kicking or scratching aimed at the offender. Did the victim say to the offender no, stop or I don't want to do this? What is the relationship with the suspect? Clarify if the offender is a stranger or a known person to the victim. What were the suspects action prior to, during and after the assault and was force used to threaten by the offender? Have you got that?"

"Yes Ma'am," replied Lucy scribbling her notes.

"These elements are necessary in addressing the issue of consent with non-stranger rapes. They can also assist in identifying potential witnesses and gathering additional evidence. Specific details about the incident will help investigating officers determine the suspect's motives and method of operation which could help link the suspect to other similar crimes. When the interview ends the investigating officer should always ask if there is any other information she wants to add or any detail she may remember. Finally, the officer should explain police procedure and the criminal justice process, so the victim can mentally prepare for what is to come. A successful interview, Sprog, is one that causes no further harm to the victim and results in obtaining invaluable information that assists in the identification and apprehension of the suspect."

Nodding, Lucy made her final notes and closed the note book.

"Okay Sprog remember, just sit and observe. Right, follow me."

Lucy spent the next four hours observing a heart-breaking rape case. She had listened to her mentor and applied the thought process as the interview played out and arrived at a conclusion.

***

Later that day Lucy was out on foot patrol. It was early evening and still light and sunny. As she passed by one of the local pubs, The Skinners Arms, she saw a handful of guys and girls enjoying a few drinks and listening to The Real Thing blasting out 'You to me are Everything' from a hand-held tape deck. Lucy was still thinking about the day's lesson and hearing the rape victim's story, when her thoughts were interrupted by a loud, pig like snorting. She tried to ignore it but the gnawing away in the pit of her stomach wouldn't allow her to. She turned back and faced a young man, with long wavy dark hair. He wore an open necked, white shirt with the collar pulled out and placed over his pale blue blazer. His matching trousers had a small, red seam on each side, button up trouser flies and a high waist band. On his head he wore a trendy, white cloth, flat cap. Lucy looked him up and down and spoke.

"Why would you make a noise like a pig sir?" Lucy looked out at his surrounding friends and the girls for support. It didn't happen.

The man started to snort loudly and then dropped down to the grass on his hand and knees and shook his head wildly and snorting even louder. The growing crowd laughed and egged him on.

"Sir," Lucy commented sarcastically, "if you're insinuating that I'm a pig then you should know that I am proud because pig stands for Pride, Integrity and Guts."

The man continued to snort wildly, now rolling on his back and waving his arms and legs frantically.

"I'm leaving now and will be returning in twenty minutes. I would suggest that you grow up and move on." Lucy turned and walked away. The man was now snorting at an unbelievable pitch much to amusement to all in the pub.

Back at the station Lucy relayed the story to a small group of fellow officers over a cup of tea.

***

'Right," said Dominic pulling out his false teeth, "Barry, go get the van."

"Sure Boss," Barry replied with a manic grin. "What about you Del, are you gonna let this slide?"

Del was a mountain of a man with a huge red beard and moustache. He stood up, shrugged his shoulders and said calmly, "So, let's do it!"

Lucy joined her three colleagues and they sped back to The Skinners Arms in the police van. Barry screeched to a halt and jumped out. The others followed.

"Which comedian thinks it's okay to take the piss Lucy?" asked Dominic cracking his knuckles.

Lucy pointed the culprit out. He stood drinking large gulps of beer and laughing loudly amongst several lads and a smaller group of girls.

Dominic, Barry and Del marched up across the green towards him. One of the lads stood up as they approached. "Sit back down sonny," said Del pushing hard against the lad's shoulders. Dominic leant forward and grabbed the startled pig impersonator by the neck. Del grabbed both his legs and Barry his arms.

"What's going on? I didn't mean anything. I was just having a laugh," he pleaded.

The officers carried him at waist height over to the adjoining church's doorway. It was to the right of the pub and out of view from the drinkers. "So smart arse, you think it's funny to take the piss with your stupid pig noises?" asked Dominic as they dropped him to the ground with a thud.

"No, no I was just messing about. I'm sorry, really sorry," he begged rubbing his arm.

"Well we don't like it when scummy little toe rags like you start showing off," said Barry with his arms on his hips. "See these," Dominic removed his false teeth. "I normally take these out when it looks like there's going to be trouble."

"Please, I am so incredibly sorry. I don't want any trouble," he implored with tears beginning to fall from his eyes.

"You see that woman police officer there," Dominic pointed at Lucy. "Well she is one of us, part of the team and we can get really upset if we feel that someone is taking the piss and making piggy noises. Do you understand me?"

"Yes, yes, yes. It's a misunderstanding. I'll never do it again. Please I am so sorry."

"Are you happy with that?" asked Dominic winking at Lucy. She nodded with a smile.

"You have no idea how lucky you are matey, because she would bite your bollocks clean off." Dominic grabbed him under his arm and frog marched him back to his seat at the pub. Del looked at the lad who had stood earlier who hunched his shoulders and held up both hands submissively.

"Thank you for your time sir," said Dominic with a grin. "Enjoy the rest of your evening."

***

When Lucy returned to her quarters she saw outside her door the remains of a children's party that had been held in the station earlier that day. Amongst the glitter and baubles was a paper hat with the words 'Creep of the Week' hand written on it in black ink. Lucy smiled and rolled her eyes. Some of her friends enjoyed teasing her about how Inspector Jessica Jones showed her favouritism.

Chapter 12

Lucy had taken a police vehicle and was travelling to a local school. One of the teachers had expressed a concern for one of the pupils and Inspector Jessica Jones asked Lucy to follow up the investigation.

"Good morning, I'm WPC Lucy Penfold. I think you're expecting me."

"Yes, good morning, I'm Miss Turner. I mean Andrea Turner. Thank you for coming. Shall we go through to the school office, It's more private."

Andrea Turner had a long lean body, short blond hair with almost boyish looks. Lucy noticed that she had incredibly long, shapely legs.

Lucy smiled. "Yes, that's a good idea."

They both sat down. Andrea had motioned the school secretary to make tea as she left the room. "Tea okay for you WPC Penfold?"

"Please, it's Lucy and yes a cup of tea would be nice, thank you."

There were a few seconds silence and then Lucy spoke. "How can I help you today?"

"Well, this is very difficult."

"No problem. Please take your time and start from the beginning."

Andrea smiled awkwardly. "I have a pupil, Robbie. He's a lovely, bright, little lad. I noticed that during the lesson that Robbie was hobbling and finding it difficult to walk. Rather than call him out I said that the class should play a game that involved removing their shoes and socks. It was then that I noticed Robbie had toe nails that were thick and black and growing under his feet. They were horrendously overgrown almost like claws. The poor little lad must have been in severe pain whilst wearing shoes. I took him to one side, away from his school friends, and said that he should ask his mummy to cut his nails. The following day I noticed that Robbie was still in pain and finding it difficult to walk properly. Again, I took him to one side and asked if he would remove his shoes and socks. I was horrified, they were torn, jagged and looked very sore. I asked Robbie what had happened. He told me," she said with her eyes closed and slowly shaking her head, "that his Mummy had made his sister bite his toe nails off."

Lucy looked up from her notes. "Are you okay?"

"I'm sorry for calling such a clandestine meeting like this but it is just awful. I didn't know what to do but I was very concerned for his well-being. He really is a lovely little chap to have in the class."

"Thank you for sharing this with us Andrea. Do you have the parents' address?"

"Yes. I do know that there isn't a father around and his mother has never attended an open meeting to discuss Robbie's performance at school." Andrea stopped talking when the secretary entered the room with two mugs of tea. They both thanked her.

Andrea went over to the filing cabinet and copied down the address. "Here, "she said folding her arms and tapping her foot. "If I can do anything, anything at all to help please do not hesitate to ask."

"I will, thank you Andrea."

Later that afternoon, once school had finished, Lucy drove to Robbie's home. She knocked on the door and was met by a tall, thin woman in her early thirties. She wore no make-up; her mousy, blonde hair was unbrushed and she was wearing men's pyjamas.

"Hello Miss Grant, I believe that you are Robbie's mum. Is that right?"

"Err, yes what do you want? What has Robbie done?"

"Can I come in Miss Grant?"

"Err, okay, come through."

Lucy entered the living room. It was spotlessly clean and there was a well-dressed, pretty young girl playing with several dolls and toys on the floor in front of the warm open fire.

"Hello, and who are you then?" asked Lucy with a smile.

"Hello, my name is Rosie."

"Well, what a smart young girl you are and with so many toys."

"Yes, mummy buys me lots of toys and Father Christmas brings me a whole sack full because I'm such a good girl for mummy."

"What a very lucky girl you are Rosie." Lucy turned to Miss Grant. "Where is Robbie please?"

"He's not here. I think he's out playing with his friends at the park," she answered sheepishly and looked down towards the floor.

"No mummy, Robbie's in the shed like he always is."

"No, no you're mistaken Rosie. He went out."

Lucy began walking towards the kitchen and the back door leading to the garden. "'Is the shed this way Miss Grant?"

"He's not there, he's out with his friends. I've already told you. You do not have any rights to be here."

Lucy opened the door and walked firmly towards the small wooden shed at the end of the garden. When she opened the door, Lucy found Robbie lying on the floor in his underwear with an old bath towel that barely covered his slight body. On the right was a dog bowl with a mixture of greens and potatoes. His school uniform had been hung up on a nail on the back of the door. Lucy turned sharply towards the mother.

"I never wanted him. I didn't ask for another bloody child and I didn't want a boy. I hate him, and I hate all men. They're all nothing more than a waste of space. We don't need men in our lives. They bring nothing but pain and heartache."

"Miss Grant, I need to use your phone," Lucy said coldly.

Lucy phoned Inspector Jessica Jones and relayed what she had witnessed. Robbie was being neglected and in real danger. Within an hour he was removed from the house to a place of safety and Social Services were informed. Lucy sat down and made all her notes. She documented the conversations, what she had seen and the environment in which young Robbie was living. There were very few clothes and not a single boy's toy in the house. The mother showed no remorse.

It was later discovered that the mother had a history of mental health issues and deep loathing of all males. Lucy had provided the court with enough evidence to make a decision. Young Robbie had been removed permanently and was very happily staying with foster parents.

Inspector Jessica Jones invited Lucy out in her bright red Triumph Stag Convertible. The pair drove out to a nice sized, detached home in a quiet, suburban, leafy avenue. At times Lucy had to hold her hat as Jessica wouldn't allow her to remove it. The house was where Robbie was now living. Jessica reached into the boot and produced a child's cowboy outfit, gun and holster.

Lucy asked, "Did you buy that?"

"That's none of your business 'Sprog' and if you tell a living soul what you've seen I'll probably kill you myself."

Chapter 13

Lucy had been called out to a block of council flats with PC Fred Turvey. Some of the residents had reported the smell of gas. The tower block housed over eighty families. Lucy knocked on door one and was given a spare key to gain entry. The lift door opened.

"I'm not going in there," said Fred, "it bloody stinks."

Lucy walked inside. Somebody had urinated and left a small pile of turds in the corner, along with a pink, shit stained handkerchief. She gagged.

"Come on we'll walk up. Its only six floors."

The pair raced up the stairs, making short work of the six flights. They stood outside the door. It had a white wooden panel at the bottom and an obscured wire meshed safety glass at the top.

"Looks like someone is at home," said Fred looking at a faint outline of a person through the glass.

Lucy knocked, waited a few seconds and knocked again. "Hello sir, it's the police can you open up please?" There was no answer and the outline didn't move.

"Knock again," motioned Fred.

Lucy knocked harder. There was still no answer. "Okay sir, we have a key. We are the police and are coming in now." There was no answer and the outline had still not moved. Lucy pushed the key into the lock and pushed the door forward. It opened just a few inches and stopped.

"This looks like a suicide Lucy. You're a bit thinner than me try and wriggle your way in and see if you can open the door."

"Oh, cheers Fred. I'll just get down on my hands and knees then shall I?"

Lucy managed to crawl through the small gap. Inside her nostrils came under attack by the smell of rotting flesh. The occupant had tied a nylon rope around his neck and hung himself from a steel bar that had been drilled into the ceiling. With time, the nylon rope had stretched, and the body lowered to the point where the head was just inches away from the door and the legs outstretched backwards. Fred managed to crawl through the space.

"Oh my god, it stinks in here. That smell is putrid, and I thought the lift was bad," he said. "Right Lucy you need to cut the rope down. We need that as evidence and it will allow us to gain proper access to the room."

Lucy found the kitchen and took a large knife from the drawer. She found a stool and stepped up on it, so she could cut the nylon cord at its base. Fred stood in front of the body. He wanted to ease it down on the ground once the cord had been cut. With each cut the body became heavier and soon Fred found it difficult to hold the weight. His knees buckled, and he found himself between the inside and outside of the apartment. With the final cut the body slammed forward pushing Fred clean out of the flat and onto his back in the hallway. The body and its full weight were now resting against the front door. Fred scrambled onto his knees and opened the letterbox. "Lucy are you alright in there?"

"What the hell are you playing at Fred?"

"Sorry Lucy, the weight just kind of threw me out the door."

"Right so now I can't get out and you can't get back in, is that right?"

"Try and move him Lucy. Maybe you could grab him by his legs and just move him a foot or so and we'll be home and dry."

"Really," said Lucy in a sarcastic tone.

Lucy stepped down off the stool and tried to lift the dead man's legs. It was no good. The weight was just too much. She was stuck with an aged, rotting corpse on the sixth floor of a council block of flats with no escape.

Fred was still watching through the letterbox. "I'm sorry Lucy I'll try and get some help."

Lucy could feel her stomach start to turn. The putrid smell was intoxicating. She began to gag and so removed herself from the hall. In the living room she found a shoe box on the table. Inside were several letters each addressed to a family member. On the top was a short note:

To whom it may concern

I'm so sorry that you had to find me this way. Please accept my sincere apologies but I had no choice. Could you please make sure that all the letters in the shoe box are posted to my family and friends. Once again, I'm very sorry. Thank you.

Yours

Bertie Rivers

Lucy sat down and thought about the dead man and what could have led him to taking his own life. It had all seemed so well prepared, so calculated and managed. Two hours had now passed by and Fred hadn't returned. She wandered over to the window and saw that two police cars were outside. Fred waved up to her and then walked around to the boot of the car. He opened it and brought out a red and white checked picnic blanket. He spread it out on the ground and patted down the corners. Lucy banged hard on the window. She tried opening the latch, but it had rusted and just bent. Fred and the other officers sat down and held up a sandwich. Fred looked up, smiled and motioned five fingers meaning they'll be up in five minutes.

Lucy struggled to find it amusing but she knew that sometimes, for fellow officers, humour was the only way to deal with deeply disturbing or traumatic situations.

Chapter 14

Lucy looked down at her watch. It was 9pm. She rubbed her hands together to generate some heat. It was bitterly cold. Patrolling the Burnt Lane Council Estate was almost always eventful. Tonight, it was different. There was no one on the streets. No arguing over the fences, drunken husbands fighting neighbours or stolen cars being raced around the streets by wayward teenagers.

Lucy spotted a young lad climbing up a drain-pipe. She ran towards the house shouting out, "Stop, stop!"

The lad slipped through the window but turned back and spoke to Lucy. "It's okay, this my house. I live here. I'm not a burglar."

"Alright, could you come downstairs please and open the front door?"

"Okay."

A few seconds later a young lad, no older than twelve, opened the grease stained timber door. Lucy looked him up and down. He wore blue jeans with worn holes at the knees and a creased off-white t-shirt.

"What is your name?"

"My name is Simon, Simon Pavey."

"Are your parents at home Simon? I'd like to talk with them please?"

"No, mum and dad are probably at the pub."

"Why did you climb through the window?"

"I was cold. It's much colder than normal and I just wanted to get inside. Am I in trouble?"

"No not at all. Did you lose your key?"

"I don't have a key. I must wait for mum and dad to come home. Sometimes I stay at a friend's house and listen to records, but my friend David wasn't at home, so I had to stay here and wait."

"How long have you been outside Simon? It's very cold."

"I came from school and when mum and dad didn't answer the door I went to David's. When his mum told me that he was at his nan and grandad's I came back here."

"So, you've been here, outside in this freezing cold since about 4pm?"

"Yes."

"I'm a police officer and my name is Lucy Penfold. Can I come in please Simon?"

Simon stood to one side and motioned Lucy in.

"How often do mum and dad go out and leave you outside?"

"Every day."

"Can you turn the lights on please Simon?"' asked Lucy with a smile as she entered the front room.

"They don't work," he said looking at the floor.

"That's a shame. How long have they been like this?"

Simon hunched his shoulders, "I don't know."

Lucy took her torch out and shone it around the room. She was horrified. The suite was threadbare with springs protruding through the cushions. The carpet was littered with stubbed out cigarette buts and crushed beer tins right across the room. The door to the kitchen was hanging from a single hinge, and had several large indentations which looked like punch marks.

"Have you eaten Simon?"

"No Officer Penfold."

"Call me Lucy, Simon. When was the last time you ate?"

"I had a packet of salt and vinegar crisps at lunch time."

"What about breakfast?"

"No, we never have breakfast."

Lucy walked into the kitchen and shone the torch light at the cupboards. There was a single oxo cube and two odd salt and pepper pots. She turned to the fridge. It was empty.

"Simon can you show me your room please?"

"Yes Lucy. I'm not in trouble, am I?"

"No, no Simon. You are very definitely not in any kind of trouble."

"Dad gets very angry if I do something naughty."

"Does he tell you off?"

Simon nodded his head and rubbed his upper arm.

"Does your dad ever smack you Simon?"

Simon lowered his head and paused for several seconds. "Sometimes, but only if I'm naughty."

He led Lucy up the stairs. There was no carpet, just the timber staircase. He led her through to his room. Lucy shone the torch around. There was no bed just a pile of dirty linen on the bare floor boards.

"Is there where you sleep Simon?"

"Yes."

"Where are your toys kept?"

"I don't have any toys. That's why I like going to David's house. He has a record player and lots cars. He even has an Action Man."

"He sounds like a nice friend Simon."

"David is a really good friend. Sometimes he sneaks me in a sandwich or biscuits and during the summer holidays we have lunch every day. His mum always leaves out an extra plate for me. They're really nice people."

"Are they friends with your mum and dad?"

"No. David's mum came around and had a big argument with my mum. They were really shouting at each other. I just stayed in my room, closed the door and held my hands over my ears."

"What happened next?"

"I started to cry. I really like David's family and I thought mum wouldn't let me go again."

"Did they say you couldn't go?"

"Dad said that I had been really naughty for talking about our family and that they were busy bodies. He said that if they come back again he would bash them both up."

"Did your dad smack you Simon?"

Lucy could see Simon was becoming visibly upset. "Yes, he gave me a really big smack and said that if I ever talked about the family again he would give me a really big good hiding."

"Is this the bathroom?"

"Yes."

Lucy shone the torch light. The toilet was unflushed with what looked like several days of bodily waste. Around the rim of the bath was a dingy green sludge. She leant down and lifted the towel from the floor but dropped it almost immediately as the torch shone on shit stains.

Lucy thought about Inspector Jessica Jones and how she had told her about situations like this. Repeatedly she had stated clearly that a child's wellbeing was paramount. Everything after that was secondary. If there was any doubt, even the slightest inkling then she should remove the child to a place of safety.

"Okay, Simon, let's go back downstairs."

Lucy removed her police cape and covered Simon. She walked back outside and stood under the lamp outside and radioed in. Within a few minutes Simon was taken to a place of safety, fed, bathed and given a warm bed. Lucy sat down and made several notes. She wanted to capture everything she'd witnessed and been told. Lucy was determined to apply all that her friend and mentor had taught her. She did not want Inspector Jessica Jones sending her back for more evidence.

It was just after 10.30pm. Jessica had already gone home. Lucy decided because of the importance of protecting Simon and applying police procedure she should call Jessica at home. Jessica told Lucy she had to write the statement tonight while it was all fresh.

Lucy found a quiet room and sat down with her note pad. Stopping just once for a cup of coffee, she finally completed 36 pages at 2.30am. Jessica had left strict instructions that she should call her once it was complete.

"I've completed the statement Ma'am I'll leave it on your desk for the morning."

"No Sprog, I want you to bring it to my home now."

Lucy drove out to Jessica's home and was met by a friend who introduced herself as Dot. Lucy had suspected, as did most of her colleagues, that maybe Inspector Jessica Jones liked girls more than men. Her thoughts had been confirmed even though Jessica introduced her as a good friend. Dot made two cups of coffee and went back to bed.

The two sat at the table. Jessica put on a pair of reading glasses and read hungrily though Lucy's statement. "Well Lucy," said Jessica removing her glasses and smiling. "I cannot believe that you can a write a statement like this with so little service time. Well done Sprog, very well done!"

***

When the case reached court the Judge commended Lucy on writing such an excellent statement. He claimed that he could see the house, smell the toilet and feel for the plight of Simon.

Simon Pavey was placed with a loving, caring foster family and thrived in his new environment.

Although Lucy's name was never revealed, her statement was used on police officer training courses by Inspector Jessica Jones as an example of what she wanted and expected from her officers when children were found at risk.

Chapter 15

"It seems like ages since we've been on patrol together," said Clare.

"I know. The days seem to fly past. What have you been up to?"

"Well you know I've been seeing Timothy?"

"Yes, I know. You've mentioned him a few times."

"It's getting kind of serious now."

"Really?"

"Yes really. In fact, we've been talking about getting married, having children and building a life together."

"That's great news Clare, I'm really pleased for you. How does he feel about you staying in the force?"

"Timothy believes that when you have children then the mother should be at home to make sure that they're properly looked after."

"So, what do you think?" quizzed Lucy.

"I agree with him Lucy. You know I've never been as dedicated as you or Laura. So, with any luck we'll be setting a date."

"If you're happy Clare then that's all that matters."

"I'm not the only one though."

"What?"

"Yes, Julie was proposed to last week. She told me last night that she plans to accept and will also be leaving the police."

"Wow, I never saw that coming. That's half the Tank Brigade leaving to get married and have babies. Next, you'll be telling me Laura's going too," she said in a joking way.

"No," laughed Clare. "I just couldn't see Laura settling down for a while yet. She's having too much fun and living life to her own rules. In many ways I admire her."

"Laura is most certainly a woman of substance."

"Hmmm… Can you smell that?"

"I just love the smell of fish and chips."

"Yeah. Me too. Shall we get some and eat them in the park?"

"We're not allowed to eat chips on duty Lucy."

"Hey," Lucy smiled, "I won't tell if you don't."

The girls entered the fish and chip shop and joined the short line.

"Hello ladies, and what can I be getting for you today?" smiled the owner. "Truncheon in batter with chips or maybe cop and chips?"

"Whatever you do, don't give up the day time job to become a comedian," said Lucy with a broad grin. "We'd like lashings of salt and vinegar on a bag of chips each please and well wrapped as we'll be enjoying your fine cuisine in the park."

The girls sat in the park and just before they opened their bag of chips Lucy noticed Inspector Blair walking towards them. "'Oh, shit it's Inspector Blair! Quick, quick hide your chips!"

Inspector Blair was an odd ball. He'd had twenty annual attempts to pass his Inspectors' exam. He was considered a bit of a pansy, a ladies' man who'd smile and pinch your face and say hello my flower. However, he took rank and position very seriously. Therefore, he expected to be saluted, affording the respect associated to his rank.

Lucy placed the piping hot chips inside her jacket and under her arm. Clare followed suit. They both winced feeling the heat against their thin blouses. The girls both got to their feet and saluted the Inspector. He stopped.

"Why hello my lovely, you must be Lucy Penfold the infamous testicle biter. How nice it is to make your acquaintance."

"Yes Inspector," Lucy smiled awkwardly.

"So, what are you doing here in the park?"

"We had heard that there was a gang of bag snatchers operating in the area sir."

The Inspector proceeded to engage them both in conversation for almost ten minutes. Finally, he said, "Well I must be off now. Enjoy your chips!"

"Why, the wry old bugger," laughed Lucy removing the still hot package. He knew we had those chips all along.'

***

Later back at the Station Lucy was called into the Superintendent's office.

"Thank you for coming in at such short notice. It has come to both mine and your colleagues' attention that you are very capable of looking after yourself. Therefore, as part of your career development you'll be drafted into a task force and posted to Newquay with immediate effect. With over twenty thousand holiday makers arriving over the summer months you'll be dealing with a wide range of issues. This is a splendid opportunity WPC Penfold for you to shine and enhance your career as a police officer. Travelling warrants have been issued for tomorrow morning. Sergeant Bob Sanderson will be leading the task force. You'll find him in the bar briefing the rest of the team."

"Thank you, Sir," said Lucy with excitement in her voice.

The Superintendent could see the pupils of her eyes widen with the shock and surprise of his words. He wished Lucy well and motioned her towards the door.

This is fantastic, Lucy said to herself punching the air.

***

Lucy found Sergeant Bob Sanderson at the bar surrounded by four officers.

"Sergeant Sanderson," she smiled, "I'm WPC Lucy Penfold. I was told that I'd find you here."

"It's just Bob, no formalities in the task force Lucy. Is that okay with you?"

"Yes Sergeant Sanderson, sorry I mean yes Bob."

"No problem. This is the rest of the team. Jim, Tony, Fatboy and Danny."

"Here Lucy," said Danny, "do you know what a man with a ten- inch penis has for breakfast?"

Lucy shrugged her shoulders and went pink with embarrassment.

"Well I normally have eggs and bacon," Danny laughed out loud. The others joined him.

"You have to forgive Danny," said Bob with a smile. "He's like a predator when it comes to the ladies. The guys are a good bunch. What do you want to drink?"

"Cheers, I'll have a whisky and ginger ale please." Bob motioned Fatboy to get the drinks in.

"So, what is the plan Bob?" asked Lucy.

"Well tomorrow morning we travel by train down to Newquay and report in to Superintendent Luscombe."

"Superintendent Luscombe," quizzed Lucy, "what's he like?"

"Newquay comes firmly under what has become known as Luscombe's law. I'll give you an example. It is not unusual to find Superintendent Luscombe sitting at the back of a court and he'll motion the judge, by holding up his fingers what he wants. I mean if it's a fine then the judge would look over and if Luscombe is holding up five fingers then it's either £50 or £500. Then if it's a custodial sentence the Judge would take Luscombe's lead and hand out the sentence. Ten fingers meant ten months and that would be that."

"I heard," interrupted Fatboy sucking furiously on his cigarette, "that he had one team dress up in shorts and t-shirts and go rattling cans on the beaches collecting for his favourite lifeboat charity."

"You think that's bad," said Jim in a sarcastic tone. "I was told that the pool table in the officer's bar had been torn and the cost was something like £400 to be repaired. Well Superintendent Luscombe gave them a choice. It was you all go down for a week and clear out the gardens of a Police house that would have normally cost around £400 from the council and have the table repaired or the table stays as it is."

"The icing on the cake has to be that when the council refused to paint yellow lines in front of the nick he had a couple PCs out there with brushes and paint." Bob paused to take a sip from his drink. "I think it's fair to say," Bob's eyes were firmly fixed on Lucy, "that Superintendent Luscombe is hard but fair.

Fatboy handed out the drinks.

"To the Task Force," said Bob raising his glass. "Cheers!" they chorused in unison.

Chapter 16

⬅——————➡

"How the hell did you lot get down into Cornwall without a passport?" bellowed Superintendent Luscombe.

"Right, I'll see you one by one, starting with you." He pointed at Lucy and motioned her into his office.

Superintendent Luscombe was lean and tall. He had the deep, grooved skin of a man who had smoked himself old before his time. His greying hair was cut short and combed over a small balding patch.

"I'm going to cut straight to the chase with you WPC Penfold. I have one other woman police officer and she is office bound and that is where you will be. Your job will be to assist her in her office duties. So that I am very clear with you. I run a very tight ship based on firm rules. As a WPC you will not be leaving the station. Is that clear?"

Although her heart was racing, she clenched her fists under the table and then raised her eyebrow as if he was a complete idiot. "Thank you for making your position crystal clear Sir, however," she continued, her eyes firmly fixed on his, "Superintendent Luscombe, there are two things that you need to know about me. I am not part of your staff. I was selected by HQ, so with all due respect I am not part of your force. Secondly, and forgive me if this sounds rude but, I spent four years in an office prior to joining the police and discovered I was anything but a stuck behind the desk office wallah. I am best on the job, being out there involved and amongst it. In time, Inspector, you will see how I work and maybe view the role of a WPC differently."

Superintendent Luscombe sat back in his chair. The atmosphere in the room was electric. He stared for several seconds and then leaned forward. "Okay WPC Penfold. I've listened to what you've said but," his eyes becoming increasingly fixed on Lucy's, "if you take just one step out of line then," he grinned nastily, "you will be out. One last thing. If you see a black in a sheepskin coat, nick him! It doesn't matter if he's fat, thin, young or old because he's probably a drug dealer."

Lucy stood and smiled nervously as he gestured her to leave, "Yes Sir, and thank you Sir." She turned at the door and faced him. "I will not let myself or you down Superintendent Luscombe."

Chapter 17

Lucy and Fatboy were walking through the town on patrol, dressed as holiday makers. Beach Boys music blared from the bars and longhaired surfers walked along carrying their boards. They had both witnessed small mixed groups of surfers sharing what was clearly a cannabis spliff.

"How are you finding things Lucy?"

"It's good, really good. Listen do you mind being called Fatboy? Would you rather I called you something else?"

Fatboy took a deep breath and smiled. "No, I'm fine with it. Don't get me wrong if someone that I don't know throws an insult then I'll react accordingly, but Bob and the lads are just good guys and its harmless banter amongst mates. Let's face it," he said jiggling his belly, "I am overweight. I do eat all the wrong stuff. I love a doughnut or two. I like three sugars in my tea and I'd rather eat dog shit than sit down to a salad."

"Err that's nasty," said Lucy slowly shaking her head.

"I'll tell you what though Lucy; Danny is having the time of his life. I think he's seeing this a more of a busman's holiday. He's been shagging anything with a pulse and a pair of tits. Sorry I mean breasts. I know that Jim has been picking him up in the mornings from guesthouses and caravan parks all over town."

"I like Danny, he's a nice guy but, in my view, he has a few self-esteem issues. He'll sort himself out."

"Yeah he'll probably get some bird up the duff and end up getting married. Either that or he'll shag the wrong housewife and end up beaten senseless and in hospital."

Lucy looked over her shoulder and spotted Bob on the other side of the road with his head buried in a newspaper. The team moved in formation to handle situations as they happened.

Lucy and Fatboy turned off the main road into the side street where she had parked the police van that morning. It led out towards the caravan sites and open countryside. From behind a tree a scruffy looking slim man with long straggly blond hair dressed in jeans and a brown stained t-shirt stepped out. Lucy's eyes were drawn to his waist. He had his penis gripped firmly in his hand and was clearly excited. Lucy stared in shock disbelief.

The silence was broken. "Well you can put that away, you sick bastard. You're nicked!" Fatboy shouted.

The flasher pushed his manhood away, turned and raced away. Fatboy gave chase. Lucy called out to Bob who was on the other side of the road just forty feet away. "Flasher, Bob. Fatboy's given chase." With that she took off.

Bob pulled out his radio and began relaying their position and a brief description into the station as he broke into a slow jog.

The flasher looked behind and cut across behind a parked car and into the road. A family travelling in a brown Austin Maxi came to a screeching stop narrowly missing him. The driver, clearly agitated, wound down the window, beeped his horn and called out "Look where you're bloody going you idiot!"

Fatboy and Lucy raced across the road, both holding their hands up in a stop motion to the driver. The flasher had gained some ground.

Ahead, he came to face to face with two middle aged women carrying shopping bags. He barged between the two knocking one to the ground. It knocked him off balance. He staggered but quickly picked up his pace again.

They were approaching a main road. The flasher didn't stop, he ran out into the coming traffic causing vehicles from both sides to emergency stop. He ran ahead into a cul-de-sac. Lucy overtook Fatboy and Bob was now only a few feet behind. They crossed the road, past the stationary traffic. They were both gaining ground. The flasher stepped out into the middle of the road and seemed to get a second burst of energy. At the end of the road was a wire link fence topped with three layers of barbed wire leading out into a field. The flasher ran, leapt and cleared the obstacle with ease. Lucy could feel the adrenaline pumping hard through her body. She grappled the fence lifting herself up and over. The barbed wire hooked in. The more she moved the harder it gripped her. Bob leapt and was over. He landed on the soft green grass, looked and looked back.

"'Are you alright?" he asked drawing heavily for breath.

"Go, go, go Bob!"

Lucy noticed a large brown horse trotting towards her. For as long as she could remember she had a fear of horses. It was the large teeth. Lucy wriggled and twisted. The barbed wire seemed to anchor her down further. Finally, she stopped and composed herself. She leant forward and took a firm hold of the wire fence, twisted to her left so that there was now more weight. Her jeans tore as she slumped to the ground in a heap. The horse stepped back, neighed loudly, turned and trotted away. Lucy was back on her feet, she reached behind her and could feel her underwear. The barbed wire had torn the back of her trousers clean out.

Looking ahead she could see that Bob was closing in. She leapt up and sprinted forward as fast her legs would carry her.

Bob could see a non-HGV green flatbed truck parked the other side of the wooden gates. The flasher was desperately racing towards it and possible escape. Digging deep Bob increased his pace. He was running on sheer determination.

Fatboy had collapsed by the wire link fence. He had slumped down on to his hands and knees gasping ferociously for breath.

Bob was only a few feet behind the flasher now. They both cleared the wooden gate within seconds of each other. The flasher reached into his pocket and thrust his keys into the door lock. As the truck door opened Bob dived, rugby tackle style, catching the flasher around the waist and bringing them both down onto the tarmac with a thud. He grappled with the flasher as he tried to slip away. Grabbing one arm he managed to pull it round behind his back. Lucy ran around by the truck and sent both knees crashing down on the flasher's shoulders. Then with both hands she pushed the base of his neck hard down into the ground. Bob produced a set of handcuffs, grabbed the second arm and secured their prisoner.

Lucy looked down on his yellow tobacco stained fingers. She could smell the stench of sweat and stale smoke.

"You mate," said Bob victoriously, "are well and truly nicked!"

***

Later, back at the station bar the task force were having drinks. "Hey Lucy, you did really well today."

"I'm a police officer Bob. It's what I do."

"I know but there are plenty that would have stepped back and left the hard work to others. Nice one Lucy. It's good to have you on the team. So, what do you do when you're not getting stuck in or biting testicles?" he laughed out loud. "Yeah we all know about that."

"I'm just putting the hours in."

"So, no boyfriend then?"

"No Bob," her voice a little sharper than intended, "and I'm not looking for one either."

"I didn't mean, well you know what I mean. I'm engaged to a girl called Mary. We're supposed to be getting married later this year."

"Oh, I'm sorry, it's just that, well it must be the uniform or something in the police tea because if someone's not trying to pat your rear or pass a suggestive remark they're blatantly trying to get into your pants. It's good that you have someone and I'm sure she's a lovely girl and you'll both be very happy together. Is she in the force?" asked Lucy diffusing the situation.

"Oh god no," he said pausing briefly to light a cigarette. "Mary is a school teacher. We've been together about five years and, well it just seemed like time to do the right thing. Although now, I'm not sure."

"What do mean, not sure?"

"Maybe I'm just scared of marriage. You know kids, a mortgage, bills and all that."

"You mean commitment?"

"I suppose so. I'm not sure that my own parents really loved or cared about each other. They fought like cat and dog but just elt that they should stay together because, well, because why? If it isn't right or you're not sure maybe you just shouldn't be together."

"Being away is a time to reflect and maybe just let your worries or concerns escalate and get the better of you. I'm certain that when you get back you and Mary will do what's best for you both."

"Keep this to yourself though Lucy. This is not the kind of conversation you have with the lads."

Lucy smiled, "Of course not, mum's the word."

"Alright you two, what are you drinking?" asked Danny striding towards them with a steely glint in his eye.

Lucy could smell instantly a mix of Brut aftershave and tobacco smoke.

"Cheers Danny, that's a Southern Comfort and lemonade for me and a whisky and ginger ale for Lucy."

Danny gestured the order to the barman.

"So, are you out on the town again tonight?" Bob asked.

Danny's eyes lit up as he smiled. "Well that depends."

"Depends, depends on what?"

"Depends on whether Lucy is going to invite me back to her single persons' quarters to sample her clean white starched sheets on my naked bum and a bit of how's your father."

"You," scorned Lucy, "are about five inches from having your bollocks lopped off without any anaesthetic."

Danny winced, laughed and made a mock grab at his crutch. "See what I mean Bob," nodded Lucy lazily.

"Yeah well," Danny grinned, "I've had a nice touch today. Red Rum has won The Grand National for the third time and I had a few quid on him to win so I'm out on the pull tonight down The Blue Lagoon Club and taking the lads with me. I mean with all these loose women just gagging for it even Fatboy could get laid. What about you two, fancy a night out?"

"Nah, not for me Danny. I'm going to see that new James Bond Movie, The Spy Who Loved Me, at the Camelot Cinema. I've always liked Roger Moore even back as a youngster when he was Simon Templar in The Saint," Bob replied.

"What about you Lucy, fancy checking out what Newquay has to offer?"

"No thanks, I'm going to have another swift one here and then go to bed. I've got some notes to write up."

Danny swallowed down his drink in one. "Right then you pair of party poopers, have a good night and I'll see you in the morning."

"Has Danny always been like that, you know the male version of a slag?" Lucy asked Bob.

"Danny, yeah. I've known him for years. We both came into the force at the same time. He thinks of himself as a bit of player. He wasn't always like that. In fact, he was engaged to this lovely looking girl called Cynthia. She was from a, well let's say privileged background. You know the type. Mummy and daddy vote conservative, drink afternoon tea and play polo at the weekends."

"Really, he doesn't look the type. What happened?"

'Well the truth of it was that they never approved of him or his working-class background and it was just that which probably attracted her to him. You know the kind of thing, this is my working-class bit of rough policeman Danny. No, she was always going to be married to one of the country-set and Danny was just a plaything along the way. Maybe that's why he is why he is, just getting his own back. I don't know. Maybe being laddish and promiscuous is his way of standing out from the rest. A way of getting attention, even recognition or adulation from his friends. It could be that it's what he does to get noticed."

"You've done it now Bob. I had written him off as a dummy whose brain rested inside his underpants. Now I'm almost feeling sorry for him and don't worry," she smiled, "I won't say anything."

Chapter 18

"Well done everyone, we've had a damn good week adding thirteen arrests last night. Superintendent Luscombe was right. A significant number of criminals with outstanding warrants or on the run make their way down to Newquay and hide in plain sight. Between us we've found them working at hotels, pubs and arcades. The hoteliers have been most helpful by allowing access, so we can carry out spot checks, searches for drugs, stolen goods or unusual large amounts of cash without the need for a search warrant."

"Cheers Bob, can we all have a rise?" Fatboy asked.

"No, but we can be sure that the people who pay your wages will be sleeping safer in their beds at night. Now on to something a little more serious. There have been three reports of rape at a holiday park during the last month. Each one of the victims has been a holiday maker. We do not have a clear description of the offender. What we do know that this man is violent and dangerous. I think there may be other crimes committed during this same time that have not been reported. From what I've read so far it looks like we're dealing is the kind of man who feels animosity towards woman and wants to punish and degrade them. He may or may not be a substance abuser. This man is impulsive and can change direction within seconds with an explosive violent temper. Our rapist could be a holiday maker, an on-site worker or a visitor. What he is doing, is looking for the opportunity to rape not for a specific victim. He has climbed in through open windows then attacks spontaneously and brutalises and beats the woman into submission. All three of the reported attacks clearly show that any level of resistance has enraged him further and caused him to inflict severe injuries. A rapist like this is not looking to kill their victim, but he has left one close to death. This is a very serious case. Our rapist is a sadist who derives sexual gratification from inflicting pain. He is almost certainly charming and intelligent. The kind of person no one would suspect. However, what we do know is that he has tied, gagged, blindfolded at least one of his victims and then tortured them over several hours. He ensures absolute control over the victim so there's no question of resistance nor escaping. From what we've been able to patch together our rapist acts in a premeditated and rehearsed manor before he carries out the attack."

There was complete silence in the small meeting room. Bob continued.

"We've been able to secure a caravan on the site for one week. The plan is to place a decoy on site in the hope that we can bait the rapist to strike again."

"Who is the bait Bob?" asked Danny.

"I'll do it," offered Lucy, "I'll play the part."

"Thank you, Lucy. I was hoping, counting on and expecting you to volunteer. All the task force will be on site undercover with night vision goggles and radios. You will be as safe as we can make you."

"Rapists are the lowest of the low," growled Fatboy.

"Yeah rapists and kiddie fiddlers they're all low life scum of the earth. They want taking out to a field somewhere and putting down," said Danny through gritted teeth.

"Well it's that or we catch the bastards and get them locked up and out of harm's way", said Bob inhaling hard on his cigarette.

"Yeah and when they've been weighed off and banged up with the hardcore of the criminal fraternity they inflict their own kind of justice. Like I said there's no place in this world for scum like that. Don't you worry Lucy, we'll be right there ready and waiting to take this scumbag down."

***

Later that evening the task force, dressed as holiday makers, positioned themselves strategically around the caravan. Lucy, dressed in a light green above the knee night dress, had wandered out onto the porchway with a mug of hot coffee. She sat outside on clear show that she was alone and potentially vulnerable and then ventured back inside leaving the door open.

"Do you read me Lucy?" radioed Bob.

"Yes, I read you Bob."

"Anything suspicious to report?"

"No, I've left all the windows and front door open. The lights are all off except the table lamp. What about you. Anything happening your end?" Lucy asked.

"No, nothing but a rabble of drunken holiday makers doing the conga dance and singing Knowing me, knowing you by Abba."

"This must feel like another normal night out for Danny."

"Oi I bloody heard that," radioed Danny.

"Don't worry Danny, you were meant to. We all know you'd shag a sheep if that was all that was available," Lucy laughed nervously.

"Yeah, Danny the sheep shagger!" roared Fatboy.

"What about just sheep shagger? Here, what would you call a sheep shagger if he had a sheep under his arm? A pimp!"

"And you can fuck off too!" retorted Danny angrily.

"Come on girls," said Lucy, "let's all make up and play nicely."

"Okay that's it now. I want radio silence and you lot to keep your eyes and ears open," ordered Bob.

***

Lucy stared up at the clock, it was just after 4am. There had been radio silence now for just over an hour, but she knew she was safe and that her colleagues were close by and ready to pounce into action. Lucy sighed and reflected on what a positive influence and mentor Inspector Jessica Jones had been. She smiled remembering the first time she had called her Sprog. Jessica had helped her integrate seamlessly and quickly into her new environment. Jessica had jump started the learning curve and helped her succeed. It felt as if Lucy had been evaluated quickly within the culture of Exeter Police. Jessica had brought Lucy in and got her involved. On a few occasions she had been taken down to listen in on rape cases. Lucy remembered and marvelled at her words before entering her first rape victims police interview.

"What you have to remember Lucy, is that a serial rapist cannot be understood with logic. A rapist will rape a woman he does not know because of the perceived injustice he suffered at the hands of a woman he does know. It could be something as simple as a girl not giving him the time of day when he was younger. It is not about the sex, but violence. Rape is about control and punishment. It is not that they need sex so badly but an overwhelming, almost uncontrollable need to control and punish others."

It was these words and the experience of sitting in on those rape victims' interviews that made Lucy volunteer as the bait.

Jessica had taken time out to articulate, make her familiar and integrate with Police culture. She had consistently demonstrated honesty, integrity and both respect for and the responsibility for stewardship. Communication between the two had always been clear and effective both verbally and nonverbally. Jessica had a wonderful way of providing feedback for both failures and successes.

Lucy concluded that Inspector Jessica Jones had a profound effect on her life and helped shape both the person and police officer she was becoming.

The sun had risen, and the bright morning light entered the room. Lucy got up of the bed and put the kettle on.

"Hello Lucy, do you read me?" It was the radio.

"I've got you Bob, loud and clear. Nothing to report for day one."

"Yeah our guy has consistently carried out his attacks well after dark, so we'll call this a day, regroup back at the nick and then grab some rest."

***

Lucy slept well back at her quarters and was back on the caravan site with the task force just before 7pm.

Lucy and Bob were alone in the car.

"Have you got everything Lucy?"

"Yeah, I'm ready."

"Good, because I really want to see this guy taken down," he paused for a few seconds. "I spoke with Mary earlier today."

"Oh good, how is she?"

"She's okay. We spoke during the children's lunch time. I told her that we need to speak when I get back."

"Is everything alright?"

"No, not really Lucy. Increasingly I'm thinking that it's a mistake and I should be stopping it all now. I'm not sure that I should really be with anyone outside the force. At least then I'd have someone to share my thoughts, problems and successes with. Mary, or come to think of it, no one outside the force would understand what it's like to attend a fatal car accident one minute, console an old lady whose been robbed the next and then nick a gang of thugs for going around bashing up queers."

"I don't know what to say Bob."

"You do understand what I mean though, don't you?"

"Look I'd like to say yes and somehow validate your thinking, but I just don't know. Right now, I'm just taking each day as it comes, staying crystal clear on nicking criminals, building relationships with my colleagues and forging a career. As your friend I'm here if you need to talk but whatever you do don't go making any rash decisions until we've wrapped up Newquay are back on our home ground."

"Sure, thanks for listening Lucy. You're a good friend."

Back in the caravan Lucy followed the same routine. She dressed in the same short night dress, opened all the windows and after sitting outside on the steps with a cup of coffee for half hour then returned inside and turned all the main lights off except for the bedside table lamp.

The dark fell and soon it was after midnight. She could hear the holiday makers singing Abba songs and laughing drunkenly as they left the club house. Bob had radioed in with nothing unusual.

Lucy began thinking about her conversation with Mandy from the knitting circle and her girlfriend Rhonda. Both had overcome a difficult relationship with their mothers. Lucy knew it had to be herself to make the first move because if left there would never be another word spoken. It was the right thing to do. She thought about how she had changed her own reactions and responses and somehow instinctively the dynamic had changed. They had both not fallen down the same route with the inevitable outcome. It had seemed to please them both and was a small but very positive step in the right direction. Lucy decided that she too should shoulder some of the blame by maybe having unrealistic expectations from their relationship. It had been refreshing, almost therapeutic. Whatever it was she knew that, albeit early days, the relationship was gaining momentum.

Lucy heard a noise. She leapt off the bed, her heart thumping, and looked out the window and saw a small fox scamper away between two caravans.

"Lucy, do you read me?"

"Yeah Bob."

"We have a suspect. A man has passed and walked around the caravan three times, each time stopping to look up at the open windows. He's milling around the front door now. We are all on standby."

Lucy could feel herself tensing up, a cold sweat raced across her forehead and her mouth felt so dry it was becoming difficult to breath. Suddenly she felt a thud to the back of her head, her knees buckled as she staggered forward. A hand grabbed her hair and dragged her violently across the room. He threw Lucy to the ground and kicked her in the stomach. Dazed, Lucy managed to stand and run a few steps. She was grabbed with overwhelming force from behind. Lucy could feel his excited, hot short, breaths on her neck. Something took over, just for a few seconds all the pain and fear left, she had clarity. Lucy leant forward and then thrust her head back hard into her attacker's face. He yelped with pain. She turned quickly and kicked him hard between the legs taking his breath away and forcing him down on his knees. Then bringing her leg back she kneed him hard in the face. Her adrenaline was racing through her veins. Her attacker reached into his pocket and produced a switch blade. As he clambered to get back on his feet Bob, Fatboy, Danny and the rest of the task force crashed through the door. The attacker was disarmed, on the floor and handcuffed in seconds.

"You okay Lucy?"

"Yeah, sure. I just feel a bit dizzy."

Danny turned the lights on.

"Fuck me Lucy you're bleeding, and bleeding bad."

"Danny, Fatboy," barked out Bob, "get this sick bastard down the nick! I'm taking Lucy to the hospital. Those are head wounds."

***

Bob got Lucy to the hospital and fortunately no stitches were needed. The serial rapist had been caught. In his caravan he had a diary that recorded eleven rape incidents in graphic detail. Each one had pushed boundaries further. Bob, Lucy and the task force had a great result.

Chapter 19

"We've been following this van for days. Anyone would think that the villains knew we were watching," said Lucy through gritted teeth.

Bob suppressed a smile and drew heavily on his cigarette. "Surveillance is a game of patience. Sometimes you can get a result quickly and then there's others you must put the time in. The lot that's nicking cigarettes, by the box, out the back the delivery vans have a good taste of quick, easy money and they're not about to stop just yet. Fags, booze and electrical goods are the easiest and quickest things to sell. These boys are making the equivalent of two or three weeks wages in thirty seconds. No, Lucy, these boys will be back. We'll just have to be patient."

"I know you're right but just following a van around day in and day out can, well you know what I mean."

"How did it go with your mum?"

"Yeah it was great seeing her and the dog was no trouble. Fatboy was a sweetheart and offered to walk it a few times."

"Where was it she went?"

"She went to Spain with my Aunt for a week and asked if I'd look after the dog. It was no trouble, just the one very minor accident but other than that, no it all went well. I may even take some time off when we get back and pay her a visit."

"Spain, I've never been. For some reason it conjures up pictures of straw donkeys and kiss me quick hats."

Lucy rolled her eyes and smiled. She thought briefly about the little silver, blue and orange Silver Jubilee plastic flag Mother had brought her. It was now on her wall. It had made her happy for she knew bit by bit they were getting closer. Finally, she spoke.

"Donkeys, hats, Sangria and hordes of drunken English yobs staggering about fighting, belching and singing, 'We're off to sunny Spain – Eviva Espana'. We'll that's the tourist parts. It's a rich, glorious country steeped in rich culture and history. It's on my list of places to visit."

"Looks like we're on the move again," Bob interrupted. He selected first gear and after a few seconds began following the cigarette van again. He looked in his mirror and saw that the rest of the task force were not far behind. Lucy leant forward and put the radio on. 'Float on' by The Floaters was playing. Bob stretched out and turned it up.

"I like this record, what about you?"

"Yeah, it's alright.'"

"What do you think about, what's it called again, Punk Rock?"

"Sounds like some demented bloke screaming down a microphone to me although to be honest I did find that record 'Peaches' by The Stranglers pretty catchy."

"Yeah I liked that track too."

"Hold up!" Lucy exclaimed. "What's going on here?" She had seen a white Ford Escort van pull in between the delivery van and them.

Bob reached down for the radio. "Danny, we may have something. Close the gap."

The delivery van stopped outside an Off Licence on the main road. The white Escort pulled in behind. Danny drove past them both and parked in front of the delivery van.

"Right, no one moves until they have the fags in their hands alright?" Bob commanded over the radio.

"Yes Guv." Lucy could feel the adrenaline start to build up. She was itching to get out there and help make the arrests after days in the car.

"Fuck me, he's a big fella!" radioed Danny. A huge mountain of a man had got out the van. He was dressed like a builder, with dungarees stripped down and tied around his waist.'

"I reckon we should leave the big fella for Fatboy to bring down, what do you reckon Bob?'" Danny asked.

"Pipe down and get ready to move the second he lays a hand on the fags."

The big fella walked to the right of the Off Licence passing the delivery man. He entered a Wavy Line grocery shop. The delivery driver got back in his van and man mountain left the shop with a pint bottle of milk. He tore off the silver cap and drank hungrily at its contents.

"Shit, it's a false alarm guys," Bob said with disappointment in his voice.

The driver returned his empty van to the yard without incident.

***

Later that evening Lucy had left the Police Station deciding to eat fish and Chips alone on the seafront. The task force would come together later that evening and plan night patrols. She wanted time to think and maybe make some plans for when she got back to Exeter. She found the sea crashing against the shoreline almost comforting. Sometimes hours could pass by in what seemed like just minutes.

Lucy stabbed the wooden fork into her vinegar drenched chips and then spotted Fatboy walking towards her.

"Hi Lucy."

Lucy nodded, her mouth full of a mixture of battered fish and piping hot chips.

He looked awkward, like there was something on his mind. "What's up Fatboy?"

"We're friends, right?"

"Yeah, of course.'

"'So, then I can trust you?"

"Trust me, with what?"

"I'm not sure how to start."

"The beginning is usually a good place," said Lucy bluntly.

"You promise not to say anything." Fatboy hesitated.

Lucy shook her head feeding her mouth a second fork full of fish.

"Look you know I'm not that good with birds, I mean women, right? It's not like I'm like Danny where woman's knickers seem to fall to their feet after just a smile."

"No, you and Danny are different. Danny's type is anything with a pulse and I suspect you're the more sensitive kind of a guy."

"Yeah, sensitive that's me. That's all well and good but when it comes to chatting up birds I just get tongue tied and, to be perfectly honest, I'm scared of rejection. You know being told that a person doesn't fancy you enough times can really affect your confidence."

"Is there someone in particular, do I know them?"

"No, it's not that. I'm a red-blooded normal bloke right and I have needs and urges just like everyone else and there comes a time when doing it yourself just ain't enough."

Lucy coughed and the choked on a hot chip. "I'm not sure I can help with this," she offered awkwardly.

"Sorry, what I'm trying to tell you is that last night I really had an urge, you know. I wanted to be in a woman's company. I wanted to hold her in my arms, kiss her lips and be intimate."

"So, what did you do?"

"I heard a couple of the stations regulars talking about a massage parlour that doubles up as a knocking shop."

"And?"

"Well I put a decent pair of trousers on and a good shirt and took a wander down there. I hung around outside for maybe ten or fifteen minutes trying to build up the courage to knock on the door."

"Did you Fatboy?"

"Yeah eventually I took deep breath and knocked. It was opened, and I was quickly ushered into a large lounge. Lucy it was wall to wall birds. I mean they were everywhere. There were black ones, Asian ones, fat ones, young ones, redheads, blondes. I mean honestly just for a second I thought I'd died and gone to bloody heaven. They were sitting around on sofas and chairs in various stages of undress. You know, stockings, nighties, bra and knickers all sorts. Some of them didn't leave anything to the imagination. It felt like all their eyes on were on me, looking at me expectantly. It was like they were waiting to see who would make the move on first. Just then I caught the eye of this gorgeous woman. She must have been in her early thirties, tall with super long legs and blond hair. She had the most amazing pair of Bristols."

"So, you went to a brothel and paid for sex?"

"Oh my god no! To be honest it started like that. I wanted to give in to my impulses and then when I saw her I knew that it would be just too cheap and tacky."

"So, what did you do then?" quizzed Lucy.

"I smiled and told her that I needed to be somewhere but that I would be back again and then left as quickly as I arrived."

"Okay, let's get this right. You go to a knocking shop and find that you have feelings for one of the working girls but don't do anything?"

"Yeah, I know it sounds silly and if it had been Danny he'd have stayed all night sampling everything on offer. I would just, well you know, like to spend some time with her, get to know her as a person and then see where it goes."

"Right Fatboy, I think It's time you stopped and took stock of where you are. Firstly, you're a police officer and going into a knocking shop, unless it's to turn it over, is a serious risk to your career. Secondly that woman or any of the others can and will be anything you want for as long as your pound note lasts. You're a punter Fatboy, nothing more. It's a supply and demand situation. You want company and they provide it in any guise that floats your boat."

"So, you don't think she'd be interested in going out with me?"

"Fatboy, wake the fuck up! No, no and no. Now I understand that you can be a little shy around woman but trying to fall in love with a prostitute is not a realistic or viable option. You have got to stop comparing yourself to Danny. You're both very different with separate issues. He has self-esteem problems and they are a lot harder to overcome than simple shyness."

She leaned forward and patted his arm. "You're a nice guy Fatboy. I think that you should be looking for a different type of woman. The chances of finding what you desire lurking about in a knocking shop or twitching about in the local disco is highly unlikely. Why don't you try joining clubs, church groups and the likes? Look for a person who can see beyond what they see. A person who will take the time to get to know you, the real person. Believe me, she is out there and is probably sitting right now chatting to a friend saying the same thing."

"I'd like to believe that Lucy, I really would. Tell me, if you and Bob didn't like each other would you have gone out with me?"

"Right, now let's stop right there," said Lucy assertively. "Bob and I are colleagues and friends no more. You and I are friends and that's it. I have no interest in a romantic liaison with any of my colleagues. We're all mates on the job, right?"

"Yeah, I'm sorry if I offended you Lucy. I would never want to upset you."

"It's not a problem Fatboy. You haven't. The next time we talk like this I want you to be telling me how you've met this amazing woman and how happy you both are, okay?"

"Sure," Fatboy sighed audibly.

"You want a chip?"

Fatboy's eyes lit up. He smiled bravely while taking a very large handful of chips.

Lucy looked at the almost empty packet and sighed. "What do you make of this surveillance job we're on?"

"I've done loads of jobs like this Lucy, it's just about putting the time in."

"What if we helped it along a bit?"

"How do you mean?"

"Well, they don't do deliveries at the weekends, right? So, what if we convince them to let us take the van out. We can go around and collect empty cigarette boxes and fill it with old cartons then purposely let the van doors remain open at delivery points. Let's see if we can bait the thieves to take a bite."

"I like it," Fatboy said excitedly. "I'm definitely in. Have you spoken to Bob?"

"No, not yet but I thought if you and I get everything together and I speak with the company, then Bob just may go for it."

"Sounds good, I'm ready to make a start whenever you want."

"Excellent. And Fatboy... ," her eyes firmly fixed on him.

"Yes?"

"No more brothels, alright?"

Fatboy gave his customary shrug.

"Right let's get back to the nick, we're due out in an hour."

***

Later that night the Task Force scored an amazing result. They had asked a local hotelier if they could search the quarters and speak with his season labour. One of the Scottish lads seemed very agitated and when questioned he threw a half empty tin of Watney's Party Seven Beer. Fatboy dodged the attack and managed to tackle him down and make the arrest. Back at the nick they learned that they had arrested Paul McIntyre and he was wanted for arson on a public house in Edinburgh which had left several people hospitalised with varying burns.

***

It was Saturday morning. Lucy had convinced the company to let them take the van and fill it with old boxes and empty cartons of cigarettes that she and Fatboy had collected. Bob had reluctantly agreed to the sting.

Lucy sat up front in the driver's seat with her hair tied up under a basketball cap. "You alright back there Fatboy?"

"Yeah, I'm ready," he replied from a hiding position behind the old boxes.

"Bob, do you read me?" Lucy radioed Bob.

"Yeah, I got you Lucy."

"We're ready to make a move and follow the same routine. So, if they're out there then we'll flush them out."

"Okay Lucy, everyone's in position and I'm on your tail," Bob confirmed.

Lucy followed the delivery driver's weekly routine, stop by stop. She got out the van and did no more than carry in a clip board and speak briefly to the people at the delivery points. She asked simply for directions so not to arouse any suspicion should anyone be following outside.

Lucy slowed down at the traffic lights when a white, flatbed, builders' style van hooted and slipped in front of her. Tapping the brakes sharply, she shook her head in disbelief.

"Sorry about that Fatboy. Some twat has just cut me up. You know what I'm sure some people get their driving licences free in a jamboree bag of sweets."

"No problem, I only hit my eye but don't worry I have another," he answered, clearly agitated.

Lucy pulled into the next scheduled stop just behind the builder's van. She got out, opened the back doors and lifted an empty box feigning its true lightweight.

As she disappeared inside the shop the two occupants from the van in front grabbed a large box each. Fatboy jumped out from his hiding place and grabbed the larger of the two by his arm. Bob, Danny and the rest of the task force raced from their positions.

Fatboy was slung from the van, he rolled across the oil stained pavement. Lucy left the shop and ran over to join her colleagues.

Bob made a grab but received a smack straight in the face. Danny let out a scream and ran in with his arms and legs punching and kicking. The smaller of the two criminals held up his arms and dropped down to his knees. Danny threw him to the ground and had him cuffed. The larger guy smiled through his unkept beard and began to roll his fists in front of him like a seasoned boxer.

"Come on then coppers, which one of you wants it next?"

Bob, Jim and Fatboy all looked at each and then ran in together. The powerful man was overcome. He was on the ground. Bob pushed his head down hard onto the concrete "You're nicked!"

The sting had been successful. The bad guys had been arrested and were on the way back to the station.

***

"You, Penfold. Get in my office now!"

Lucy was ushered into Superintendent Luscombe's office. Bob tried to follow her in.

"Not you! If I want you or any of your maverick bunch then I'll bloody ask." He slammed the door behind him.

"Right, sit down WPC Penfold. I think it was big mistake letting you out. What the hell do you think you were playing out there?"

"I don't understand, we got a good collar."

"Have you not heard of agent provocateur?"

"Agent who? I don't know that name Superintendent."

"Don't they teach you anything at training college? Agent provocateur, WPC Penfold, is a person who acts to entice another person to commit an illegal or rash act to falsely implicate them in breaking the law so that they can be convicted. In short, pretty much everything that your sting set out to do."

"I'm sorry sir, I didn't know."

"So, you're sorry?"

"Superintendent Luscombe, had I known that then I would not have set out to catch the robbers that way."

"Really?"

"Yes Sir. Will this affect the arrest?"

Superintendent Luscombe sat back in his chair. He paused for moment before lighting up a cigarette and exhaling the smoke towards the ceiling. He leant forward with the slightest glint of a smile. "Fortunately, when I saw this lot being processed I despatched officers, with search warrants, to their homes. My men found evidence of stolen cigarettes, alcohol and several pounds of cannabis. It looks like this lot were major suppliers of the drug. So, in answer to your question. No, this will not affect any conviction but only because of what we found."

"That's fantastic news Sir!" said Lucy with her beaming white smile. She was apoplectic with delight.

"It's Lucy isn't it?"

"Yes Sir."

"Lucy," he said taking a deep breath and slowly shaking his head warily, "don't do anything like this again." He smiled and then laughed out loud. "My god girl you've got some spirit, now go on, away with you and, I repeat, don't do it again."

Lucy left the office, shutting the door gently, her mind still racing. That was a genuine harsh smack on the bum followed by a hug from The Superintendent. She stretched her arms over her head and wriggled in positivity and happiness as she surveyed Newquay police station and all its occupants around her.

A girl has got to do, what a girl has to do, Lucy thought to herself.

Chapter 20

The blue Transit van trundled its way down towards Newquay. The Transit had always been a favourite mode of transport for the villains. It was light, had space to store goods or people and drove and handled like a car when the need arrived. Roy Fletcher and Charlie Vaughn were on their way to pull a job.

They were both from Bristol although Roy spent an increasing amount of time in London with his cousin Vinnie. Charlie was in his teens and had been stealing cars and committing burglaries since leaving school at the age of fourteen. He had been asked by Roy to get him the Transit van, change the registration plates and help with the Newquay job. Roy was a seasoned, career criminal in his late twenties. He had been robbing warehouses, shops and vehicles in transit for almost a decade. Each job had been just that little bit riskier, with just the right amount of temptation to push the boundaries further. For Bristol and the council estate where Roy lived with his wife and two children he was at the top of his game. A local face, someone to be looked up to. However, when he started seeing more of Vinnie, his cousin, in London he quickly realised that up there, in the smoke, he was nothing. He looked at Vinnie in his hand made suits from Savile Row; beautiful, hand cut, leather shoes and crisply starched shirts. Vinnie looked more like a film star when he was out on the town. Others in the pub or clubs would look the same; their wives could have been starlets and when they weren't around the readily available woman were red hot, rampant sex on legs.

Vinnie was standing on the pavement, contemplating; top of the criminal underworld affording respect from everyone who mattered. He was an armed robber.

Roy had been afforded some respect by local villains as family, but he already decided that this was the life he wanted. He had to develop a plan. He had seen what success looked like and he wanted it so much he could feel it gnawing away at the bottom of his stomach aching to become fruition. It was on a boozy visit that Roy had been introduced to Freddie the Fence, one of London's most notorious movers of stolen property. Freddie was minted and knew everyone. Unlike most villains he wasn't border bound. Freddie did as much work in The East End as he did in South London. If a crook had goods for sale, then Freddie would know who was in the market and what they'd pay. It was over a beer that Freddie told Roy how quickly electrical goods sold and that he possessed a never-ending list of wants. Days later, when he was back in Bristol he'd come across information about a warehouse full of gear in Newquay.

Roy couldn't believe his luck; no alarms, no security and he had a ready-made customer to take everything he could deliver. Roy's dreams of moving up to London could soon become a reality. Vinnie would set him up with a smart little flat on the manor, the money from the Newquay job would get him a hand-made suit, furniture and a Jaguar. The Jaguar was important, nothing made the villain look more successful than a well-groomed MK2 Jaguar. The plan would be to have Vinnie bring him on the firm. Make him part of the inner circle. It would be banks, post offices, security vans and shooters. He had often closed his eyes and imagined how it would feel to walk into the pub and be a real face, one of the top faces. The wife and kids would be fine, he told himself. I'll leave them a few bob and send money down when I can. He remembered Vinnie smiling and telling him over brandy at a late-night club that until you've had a good high-class London brass, you just haven't lived. Sex before that is little more than masturbation without the payoff.

Roy had played the images so many times in his head. Strutting around the City like a prince, throwing handfuls of £10-pound notes down on the bar and buying everyone in the pub a drink. They would raise their glasses and cheer him. The beautiful, sexy, women would look upon him with lust in their eyes, minds and bodies. They would want and desire him and when the deed was done, he would roll off their sweating bodies and marvel at their pretty young faces then reassure himself of his usefulness to woman.

"So, how do we know the place ain't got an alarm Roy?"

"Good inside information Charlie, and that's all you need to know my old son."

"What do reckon we could score for the job?"

"Fuck knows Charlie, it'll depend on what's there. However, I have been reassured that it's a job worth doing. We'll be in, out and on our way up to London for payday."

"And your guys, good for that kind of money?"

"Charlie, my old son, Freddie the Fence is London's number one fence. He'd have our lot and forty trailers filled to the brim too and still have enough in his sky to buy the pub a drink."

"Sky? What's a sky?"

"Sky rocket, pocket. It's just a bit of rhyming slang. All the boys talk like that in London. For example," he laughed, "I might say light us a fag you Toby."

"Toby? I'm Charlie. I don't understand." "Toby, Toby Jug means mug"

"Bollocks! I'm no mug and you've only just started talking with all this London slang stuff in the last few months."

Charlie took out two Player No6 cigarettes and lit them both. He handed one over to Roy.

Roy took a deep draw and started to feign a choke. "What the fuck is this cheap shit?"

"It's a Players No6. I've always smoked Players No6 and come to think of it so have you."

"No, you're wrong there Charlie. I favour the smooth silky nicotine from a Benson & Hedges and a gold cigarette box with a matching lighter."

"Since when?"

"Since I bloody said so."

"You're really taken with London aren't you Roy?"

Roy closed his eyes, he could feel the images sending pleasure to his senses. "You wouldn't understand Charlie. London is the Capital of the universe. It is where everything and anything is possible if you know the right people. I mean if you want to bed two women at the same time or go to a party where couples just go and fuck each other's brains out then London is it."

"No way! Two women and full on orgies?"

"Yep, seen it and sampled the goodies too," Roy lied. "That's not all, it can be non-stop parties, twenty four hours a day, seven days a week when you know the right people. In the clubs you can be rubbing shoulders with film stars, actresses, the rich and villains at the top of their game. All talking millions from robberies, property deals or from the next big movie."

"So, you're definitely going to London then?" "Abso–bloody-lutely Charlie my old son."

Roy stopped the van outside the trading estate. "Right Charlie, see that warehouse over there?"

"Which one?"

"Smith's Electrical Wholesalers."

"Got it."

"Get yourself over there, check it out and find a way in. Window, door, roof I really don't care just break in and get the main door open. The quicker we're in and loaded up the quicker we're out of here and on our way to a big stack of pound notes."

Charlie, smiled. "Right, I'm on it!"

Roy watched him scamper across the yard. He stopped at a ground floor window, looked up and down the empty estate several times and then pulled out a Jemmy bar from under his jacket and began going to work on the window. Within seconds it sprung open and he wriggled through the gap and was inside. Roy started the van and pulled it round in front of the roller shutter door. He reversed up, jumped out, ran around and opened the Transit's rear doors. The roller doors were raised.

"Nice one Charlie, well done mate."

"Roy, this place is stacked out."

Roy surveyed the area. There was pallet racking from floor to ceiling and each bay was full.

"Fucking yes, we have hit the jackpot my old son!"

"Where do we start Roy?"

"Only high value goods okay? We want cassette decks, portable cassette players, transistor radios and, if you can find them, microwave ovens. Freddie reckons he orders from cafés and restaurants all over London for them and they'll pay top dollar too."

Roy and Charlie ran around checking the racks and once they grabbed what they wanted they began loading the van.

Out on the main road an old man walking his dog looked over at the open doors and old blue Transit van. He took out a pen from his pocket and scribbled the registration number on his hand. He sensed something wasn't right. In all his years living in Newquay and walking the dog along that same route he had never once seen a van working on a Sunday. The old man picked up his pace and scurried home. He would phone the police and share his suspicions.

Roy and Charlie loaded the last few boxes. The van was full to the top. Roy was only disappointed that they hadn't stolen a bigger van or maybe a truck. Every box represented a stack of money and would take him one step closer to making his dream become reality. Charlie closed the van's doors and locked them tight. "There's got be a right few grand in there Roy."

"Don't you worry about that my old son, you will be well and truly looked after."

"You want one of these cheap and nasty Players No6 Roy, since you don't have any of those flash fags you claim to like or a gold lighter to light them with?"

"Oi you, don't start getting all mouthy or we'll fall out!" "Come on I'm just having a laugh, you want a fag or not?"

"Sure, thanks. In a few hours we'll be drinking champagne at one of the clubs with my cousin Vinnie. You just make sure you behave yourself alright because up in the smoke people are called to account for their words and actions. It ain't like the council estate back home where someone might get a smack in the mouth or something. No, these boys will fucking blow your head off with a sawn-off double barrel shotgun for just not showing the right amount of respect."

"All I want is my share of the money Roy. I have no interest in London gangsters. I like the estate, I have good friends, girls that I like and a life that makes me happy. No mate, you can keep the bright lights of London. That just ain't for me. I'll take my share and be on the last train back down to Bristol."

Roy shrugged his shoulders. "Your loss mate."

Roy started the van and drove down to the main road. In his side mirrors he saw what looked like a police car in the distance. "Shit, I think we have the Gavvers behind us."

"What the fuck are Gavvers?"

"Police, cops, Old Bill, The Filth. Is that clear enough for you?"

Charlie looked in mirror. "They don't have any lights on and don't seem to be rushing so maybe it's nothing. Just keep driving and stay within the speed limits."

Roy wriggled his fingers and gripped the steering wheel. He watched the police car move closer and closer.

***

Inside the police car the officer radioed in. "I'm on the suspect vehicle's tail Sergeant. The registration is Sierra, Mike, Echo, 8, 5, Hotel. Please run a check."

Minutes later the officer got his reply.

"Sierra, Mike, Echo, 8, 5, Hotel is a 1970 Cortina 1600E."

"Thank you, Sergeant. I'm definitely tailing a blue Transit van. I'll stop them and check their documents."

The officer turned on the lights and siren.

Roy shook his head and gestured furiously. "Fucking Old Bill! Well plod I ain't about to go back to the clink for you or anyone else!"

Charlie grabbed the seat belt and strapped himself in. Roy dipped the clutch pedal and slammed the gearstick down into second gear and floored the accelerator. The Transit responded immediately, despite being fully loaded.

"Sergeant the Transit is trying to get away. I'm in pursuit. Alert other patrol vehicles in the area."

Roy slammed the Transit into third gear and held the revs high. The Transit raced through the side roads and kept a good distance. Ahead the traffic lights were changing to red. Roy held his foot down, Charlie closed held his hands over his eyes and the van shot across the junction. A motorcyclist braked, locking his front wheel and sending him over the handlebars narrowly missing the front of the van. A second car swerved to miss the injured rider and mounted the pavement knocking down an old wooden bus stop shelter.

***

"Sergeant, we have carnage at Rectory Road traffic lights. Can you please send an ambulance. The suspect vehicle is travelling at speeds in excess of 70mph and has a total disregard of the highway laws."

Roy looked in his side mirror and saw the police car had stopped at the lights.

"Right we need to find somewhere to lie low for a few hours, a farm or something. Then we can change the number plates and get back on the road to London."

As the Transit passed a junction a second police car took pursuit with lights flashing and siren wailing.

"I don't bloody believe this, fucking Old Bill!' Roy was vociferous in condemnation of authority. Once again, he rammed the stick down into second gear and launched the Transit into race mode. The police car was a lot closer, bobbing and weaving on the rear doors. "Hold tight Charlie!" Roy shouted angrily. He dipped the clutch and braked hard. The police car rammed hard into the rear doors. Its radiator exploded with steam with shots of hot water gushing out as it came to standstill. "Wahaaa, that fucking stopped you plod!" Roy shrieked victoriously.

"Fuck me Roy, you are the Guvnor, number fucking one get away driver!"

A third police car took up the chase, only now Roy was feeling confident. He would show the Newquay Old Bill what it was when you came across a real villain. No one would stop Roy from achieving his hopes and dreams. He would dine out on these stories with London's top faces for years. Roy spun the steering wheel hard and mounted a slope in the kerb. He was on the pavement with just inches either side of the speeding van. Ahead he saw an opening, an open square leading to the shopping centre. He raced across aiming for a clearing. The police car was losing pace but still in pursuit.

Just a few streets away WPC Lucy Penfold was out driving with an ageing Inspector in a Morris Minor Panda car. She could hear the commotion on the radio.

"Sergeant, this is WPC Penfold. I'm in Bridge Street by the traffic lights."

"Penfold, the suspect is driving the wrong way down a one-way road. He should be within view in minutes."

"Thank you, Sergeant. I'm on it."

Lucy raced the little car along the road, screaming through each gear with lights flashing and sirens wailing. The Inspector wrapped his arms around his seat belt. Lucy could see the van careering down the road narrowly missing parked vehicles. She grabbed the radio.

"There's a panda car coming towards us Roy!" screeched Charlie.

"I ain't stopping Charlie. It's them or us and it ain't gonna be us!"

"Sergeant, permission to ram the on-coming vehicle," radioed Lucy.

There was a second or so of silence.

"Sergeant, I need permission to ram this Transit van now!"

"Go ahead Penfold."

Lucy braced herself and thrust her foot down hard onto the accelerator. She kept her position on the road. There was nowhere for the van to escape.

SMASH!!!!!

Lucy had ploughed the Panda deep into the driver's front wing as Roy tried to swerve. The van was at a standstill. Both the driver and passenger were injured. Lucy leapt from the crashed car and ran around to the driver's door with her handcuffs. She cuffed a dazed Roy to the steering wheel before running around the van to Charlie who began stirring. She opened the door and he fell out onto the pavement. The pursuit vehicle had caught up and the officers quickly cuffed Charlie and had him bundled into the back of the police car.

"Are you okay Sir?" Lucy asked the Inspector.

"Yes, my dear. What about you?"

"I'm fine Sir. Thank you."

"That was damn fine police work WPC Penfold. In all my years I've never witnessed or been part of anything quite like that. Well done."

"Thank you, Sir."

Chapter 21

In December 1976 came a defining point in music and British youth culture. The Sex Pistols appeared on The Today programme hosted by Bill Grundy. In a bid to prove that Punk Rockers were little more than loud mouthed yobs he goaded Johnny Rotten and other band members to swear, and at one point stated that they were more drunk than he was. Bill Grundy lost his job and The Sex Pistols and Punk Rock was catapulted into the public arena. The growing punk scene had political and economic roots. The British economy was in poor shape and unemployment was at an all-time high. England's youths were angry, rebellious and out of work. They festered strong opinions and had a lot of free time. The media were driven into a moral panic as the punk lyrics commented on society and politics. Their words challenged the prevailing orthodoxies and in turn the music industry. They questioned social and political hierarchies and the notions of personal identity.

Youths would buy clothes from charity shops, mutilate the fabric and then re-fashion in a way to attract attention; shirts with frayed edges, defaced prints torn with zips, and safety pins designed to shock those outside the scene. Trousers were deliberately torn; Doc Martin boots and chains holding items of clothing together bondage style. Facial body piercings with studs and pins in eyebrows, cheeks, noses and lips became symbols. Punks, male and female, fashioned spiked hair held rigid with a sugar water solution or PVA glue. Some areas of the skull were shaved to look intimidating.

Johnny Rotten, The Sex Pistols and Punk Rock struck fear into the establishment as their ideology broke out across the face of Britain like an air borne virus.

With nihilistic singles including Anarchy in the UK, God Save the Queen and violent performances, the local authorities banned The Sex Pistols from playing in their town or cities right across the UK. They were considered a danger to the very fabric of society. Johnny Rotten hatched a plan with fellow band members to tour the UK under the band name the S.P.O.T.S which meant 'Sex Pistols on Tour Secretly.' It was an opportunity for their latest band member Sid Vicious to gain experience on bass and play to their rapidly expanding fan base. The growing army of punk rockers were desperate to find the venues and often travelled many miles on little more than a rumour.

It was late August 1977 and a small group of punk rockers, from London, had heard the S.P.O.T.S were playing in Newquay.

Regulars on The Kings Road; Chelsea, Rick, Tom, Micky, Suzie and Dawn were driving down to Newquay in a silver Ford Zodiac MK4. Suzie had taken the car keys a few days earlier without permission as her parents were away on holiday. It was her plan to have the car returned before they arrived back home, and no-one would be any the wiser. Rick was the self-appointed leader of the small group and designated himself the driver.

"So, what do you reckon Rick, are we on tonight or what?" asked Tom with excitement in his voice.

"I've told you Tom, all I know is that bird Christine was hanging out with Malcolm McClaren at his shop SEX and she said that the Sex Pistols were touring the coast under the name S.P.O.T.S. and then she heard Newquay. So that's just about it. I know for a fact that we missed a gig in Plymouth where they played under the name The Hamsters, so it makes sense that they could be in Newquay."

"Do you reckon they'll be touring with The Clash like they did last year on The Anarchy Tour?"

"I don't know. I like The Clash, but The Pistols are it for me," stated Rick

"Yeah, Johnny Rotten is just the man. He's like a gobbing machine just spitting out at everyone in the audience. Its fucking amazing."

"Suzie, you look amazing,'" said Rick his eyes looking at her reflection in the rear-view mirror.

"Thanks, it was Dawn that done my hair with pink dye and stuff. She made a right good job of it," she answered smiling.

Dawn made a loud tutting sound and shook her head.

"Sorry Dawn, you look fucking anarchic too," said Rick trying to be diplomatic.

Rick had a thing for Suzie ever since he first saw her in her punk outfit, at a Christmas party. He'd never even looked at her before believing she was a plain Jane, an also ran, but the first time he saw her in her little black shorts, black fishnets and torn black t-shirt he was spellbound. Suzie had pogo danced around the living room to Anarchy in the UK. She had looked amazing, her spiked hair staying perfectly in place. She launched into the air, collided with another dancer and crashed into the Christmas tree. She rose covered in fairy lights and began laughing hysterically. He moved forward to help her up but was beaten by her friend Dawn.

Rick didn't like Dawn. He thought of her as the ugly friend whose always there just milling around being miserable. He'd scratch his head sometimes and wonder why all the good-looking girls insisted on having ugly mates. The lads had offered up that was how they looked better because they were sitting next to a munter.

"I heard that one of The Clash has been banged up, you know sent to prison, for shooting racing pigeons with an air pistol. So, chances are they won't be supporting them," said Micky snorting loudly and then spitting out the window.

"That's fucking disgusting Micky!" said Dawn thrusting her pointed finger into Mickey's chest.

"Do that again and I'll throw you out the fucking car," Mickey retorted.

"Oh, so you're a big, hard man now Mickey? You're a middle class toss pot playing at being a punk rocker just to get a reaction from mummy and daddy. You may look the part but you're still nothing more than a spoilt little kid dressed up like an anarchist. Let's get right shall we Micky, it wasn't that long ago you were still listening to Slade."

"Come on Dawn. Leave it out. He only spat out the window for fuck sake. I mean if it was Johnny Rotten spitting you'd probably have an orgasm or something," Rick commented.

"No, I bloody wouldn't Rick. I don't like spitting. I think it's bloody disgusting. I like, no I love the music and all the energy that goes with it, but spitting is a no no."

"Come on people, we're on our way to see the greatest band in the world right now," said Tom sucking on his cigarette.

Dawn offered a smirk that clearly regarded Tom with some contempt.

Mickey picked up the July edition of Melody Maker and buried his deep into the articles. The front- page headline read: Teds versus Punks. He could feel the menace building in his stomach but swallowed the retort he was longing to give.

"I've got a copy of Sniffing Glue in the back somewhere if you want it Mickey," said Tom trying to break the growing atmosphere.

"Cheers mate. Here do you know how Sniffing Glue got its name?"

"No, how was that then?"

"Well apparently, it was named after a Ramones single, 'Now I wanna Sniff Some Glue'," Mickey explained.

"I'm not a big fan of the Ramones. I'll tell you what though. I went to The Roxy Club last week. It was only a quid to get in and there were three bands playing. Generation X, The Damned and X-Ray Spex. It was fucking great, I mean really top dollar." Tom grinned.

"The Damned are bloody brilliant. I love their first single 'New Rose'. The drumming is just amazing. It's a real distinctive sound and just gets you going."

"I like X-Ray Spex," said Suzie enthusiastically.

"Yeah, they're a great band Suzie," said Tom. "I think the only problem is that some of these new groups just sound, well you know, the same. The originals are always best. That's The Sex Pistols, The Clash and The Damned."

"I like The Boomtown Rats too," offered Suzie.

"Nah, I can't go with that Suzie," said Tom shaking his head. "They're bloody sell outs. They ain't real punk, just another band that sold out their roots for money."

Suzie shrugged her shoulders and lit a cigarette.

Tom continued, "I left school with plenty of qualifications and there's no fucking jobs. I have a right to work, to have money in my pocket, to make choices. I'm entitled to feel some self- respect. The whole western world is a joke. Society has problems, big fucking problems but they're just being pushed under the carpet by the politicians and the people who make the big decisions. It makes me angry. It makes me want to hit out. That's what punk is to me. The music is more than just a sound, it's an ideology and one I sign the fuck up to."

Dawn smiled at Tom and nodded thoughtfully.

"All sounds good Tom, but me, well I just like a good pogo, knock a few people about and if there's a tear up even better," said Rick shooting a menacing grin.

"Yeah, do you remember that group of Teddy Boys giving it the big one on The Kings Road? Strutting about in their drape jackets, drain pipe trousers and brothel creepers. What was it he had stitched on the back of his jacket?" asked Mickey looking euphoric.

"King of the Jive, I think," said Tom.

"Yeah, he started giving it large and you just decked him and his gobby mate. No talk, nothing just three hard smacks and it was all over, spark out. He was king of the fucking pavement," laughed Mickey.

"I fucking hate Teds! I mean what's all that about dressing up in the same gear your old man was wearing in the 50s. Nothing but a bunch of wannabe, Brylcreem wankers." Rick lit a cigarette and handed the packet of Players No6 to Mickey. "Mods, Rockers, Hippies and Teddy Boys don't mean anything to me. Nothing but boring old men's stories from a bygone era," he nodded smiling coldly.

They arrived in Newquay and parked the car in a side road.

Rick had short spiked blond hair with a shaved blue dyed line around his ear. He wore black leather trousers, black Doc Martins boots, a silver studded belt and matching wrist band. His Union Jack vest had frayed tears held together with safety pins. Around his neck he wore a thick chain with a padlock. He was a well-built, menacing figure, handsome in a brutal sort of a way. He slipped his black sunglasses on and surveyed all around him.

Suzie wore a light green knee length dress, which was covered in badges, and black ankle boots. Dawn wore blue faded and ripped jeans, Doc Martins and a white t-shirt with The Queen sporting a safety pin through her nose and the words God Save the Queen in black print. Suzie wore thick black eyeliner and matching lipstick. Tom wore an old black suit he'd bought from a charity shop, with a red tartan shirt that he'd ripped and sewed zips in. His hair had been cut short, dyed orange and spiked with PVA glue. Mickey wore black jeans, work boots and a blue jean vest that been covered in patches and badges. His dyed black hair had been spiked out like three hands on a clock.

The London Punk contingent had arrived. "Mickey."

"Yes Rick."

"Mark the spot."

Mickey pulled out a tin of red paint spray from under his vest and walked over to the brick wall opposite the parked car and began spraying. He stepped back and admired his work. It read: Don't Be A Slave to The System! with an offset Anarchy symbol.

"Nice one Mickey," said Dawn grinning.

Rick gave a slow heavy laugh of appreciation.

An old man, in his late 70s, looked on disapprovingly. Mickey turned his back to the man, undid his trousers, pulled them down with his pants both to his knees, exposing his bare bum and proceeded to smack each cheek. He laughed hysterically.

The group followed Rick. Holidaymakers stepped aside; one child stopped to stare but was quickly swept up and moved on. They passed several pubs that were playing loud Beach Boys and Surf music. Finally, they stopped at The Kings Arms. It was an older, run down pub. The Punks walked in. Rick smiled broadly when he spotted a group of twenty punks sitting in the corner. They followed him in.

Handing Mickey a £10 note Rick said, "Do the honours please mate." Rick nodded to the punks and approached the table. "Alright, you lot down here looking for the S.P.O.T.S?"

"Nah mate, you missed that one. They played last night at The Winter Gardens in Penzance," said the larger of the bunch.

"Oh bollocks! No fucking way! You're joking!"

"Sorry mate, they were billed as 'A Mystery Band of International Repute'."

"Gutted mate, by the way I'm Rick," he then proceeded to introduce his friends.

"I'm Des." They shook hands.

"Were they good?" asked Mickey.

"Mate they were fucking great and their new bass guy, Sid Vicious, is something else. They only played for ten or fifteen minutes but it was worth the trip."

"So, what are you lot doing here?" Rick questioned.

"Dave's parents," Des pointed to a lad at the back sinking a pint of lager, "have a caravan here so he nicked the keys and we're gonna hold up there for a few days. There's an up and coming Cornish band called The Rats," he paused to take a large gulp from his pint glass, "and they're supposed to be playing in here tomorrow night."

"Well we might as well plot up here then if that's alright with you lot?"

"Sure, grab yourselves a seat."

***

Two days earlier WPC Lucy Penfold had been called into Superintendent Luscombe's office.

"Well done Penfold, I've been really impressed with your performance here. I think you're beginning to change the way I view woman police officers."

"Thank you, Sir."

"Dare I say it, but I think I shall miss you when you're gone."

"Thank you, Sir. I'll certainly miss being away from Newquay. The summer months have been an education. There is one thing you could do Sir."

"And that is?"

"Well, it's WPC Debbie Faulkner."

"What about her?"

"Sir I believe she is capable of a lot more than the admin work she deals with."

"What are you suggesting?"

"Sir, maybe she could do some real policing, getting out and about with the public."

Superintendent Luscombe stroked his chin and paused for several seconds.

"Sir," Lucy continued, "I had someone really push me, they helped me go much further than I thought I could go. You could be that person for WPC Faulkner sir. You could give her the opportunity to grow into a great police officer."

The Superintendent leant forward with a steely glint in his eye. "I'll tell you what we can do. WPC Faulkner can go out with you and only you. She will be your responsibility and I will hold you accountable. Do you understand me Lucy, is that acceptable to you?"

Lucy beamed, "Yes Sir, that's great news and don't worry we will not let you down."

"Right then WPC Lucy Penfold, on your way then," he smiled. Lucy left and went to find Debbie and share the good news.

***

Back at The Kings Arms two hours and several pints had passed. A resident DJ arrived and began setting up his decks. Each time the story of The Sex Pistols was told it became more and more embellished. Rick and the others were gutted but took solace being amongst kindred spirits.

The pub doors swung open and several laughing lads entered. They were dressed in a mix of coloured Edwardian style drape jackets with custom coloured collars, cuffs and drain pipe trousers and crepe soled shoes. Their hair was greased smartly into a high front quiff and a tailored back. They were Teddy Boys.

"Fuck me!" said Rick to the others in a low tone, "It's Showaddywaddy."

The Teddy Boys strutted towards the bar. Shielding his mouth one of the lads whispered to another of the lads. He left the pub shortly after.

"You know where he's gone, don't yer?" said Rick with eyes firmly fixed on the group.

"Yep, reinforcements," answered Mickey nervously.

***

Two streets away Lucy and Debbie were out in plain clothes and patrolling the busy streets. Debbie pointed out the fresh graffiti saying that she had been at the fish and chip last night on the corner and it wasn't there then. They continued their walk, occasionally Lucy would radio in to Bob and the rest of the task force.

Lucy spotted a car with several lads crammed into the back seat pull up outside The Kings Arms pub. She could sense something wasn't right. This wasn't a bunch of guys going out for a few drinks and a laugh. They appeared stern faced and focused.

"Debbie hold back a moment."

They waited a few moments and then Lucy motioned Debbie to follow her into the pub. Debbie could feel a sudden surge of trepidation in her stomach but tried to ignore it. Lucy felt the tension immediately. There were over twenty-five punk rockers at one end of the pub and group of twelve Teddy Boys at the opposing end. The barman's hand trembled as he handed Lucy two cokes. The DJ looked visibly concerned as he fumbled through his record collection. He looked at the barman and shrugged his shoulders sheepishly.

"I'm just going to the Ladies, just keep an eye on them Debbie."

"Sure, no problem," she said in a low determined whisper.

In the toilet Lucy sat in the cubicle and radioed in. "Hello Bob, do you read me?"

"I read you Lucy, what's up?"

"Debbie and I are in The Kings Arms. It looks like it may get nasty. We have two large groups of youths."

"Okay, we'll be with you shortly."

Lucy returned to Debbie at the table and winked reassuringly.

Dawn got up and headed to the bar. A Teddy Boy joined her.

"So," he said smirking, "what are you supposed to be then? A boy, girl or some kind of third sex?"

Dawn turned and faced him. She stepped back and sternly looked him up and down. "What, did they bring Elvis back from the dead? Why don't you go fuck yourself, you fucking retard!"

The Teddy Boy looked shocked.

Dawn spun round and walked back to the table with a tray of drinks.

Once the shock of Dawn's curt reply sank in he glared at the punks and returned to his table. The lads gathered round, occasionally looking out at the Punks.

Dawn reached into her bag and produced a record single and then strutted pass the Teddy Boys and over to the DJ. "Can you play this?"

"Errr," he replied taking a deep breath and a sigh, "what is it?"

"Quality music, that's what," said Dawn stubbornly thrusting the single into his hand.

Reluctantly the DJ slipped the record out its sleeve and placed it onto the turntable.

'White Riot' by The Clash blasted out of the speakers. Several of the Teddy Boys pulled faces and placed their hands over their ears. The Punks rocked their heads up and down violently. Dawn stood in front of the table and began jumping up and down shaking her head. Suzie and three of the other girls got up and joined her. They all bounced around shaking their heads and waving their arms. Dawn looked over at the Teddy Boys. With clenched fists they glared back.

She snarled and stuck two fingers up silently mouthing, "Fuck off!"

When the track finished, one of the Teddy Boys, dressed in a pale blue drape suit, stood up briskly and walked over to Dawn.

"Who the fuck do you think you are talking about Elvis like that you slag!"

Dawn reached for her glass and calmly threw the contents into his face. "Me, Dawn the Punk, that's who I think I am!" she said triumphantly.

The Teddy Boy wiped his face and then stepped forward and threw Dawn to the ground. Mickey stood up and threw a punch. He missed. The Ted sent a right hook which connected and had Mick sprawling down on the floor. Several of Teds stood up. Rick was on his feet. He slipped off his neck chain with the padlock and wrapped it rapidly around his knuckles. His right arm shot out like a cannon, the cold chain link steel smashing against temple, ripping skin, cracking bone and sending blood splattering across the beer-stained carpet as he fell to the floor. The Ted was out cold. Rick then buried his black Doc Martin boot into the stomach of his victim. This was Rick's territory, he was taking a lead in this conflict. A second Ted swung a punch, which missed. Rick turned and booted the lad straight between the legs. The Ted crumpled and fell to the floor curling up into a ball. With an insane grin on his face Rick faced the remaining Teds and held both arms out by his side.

"Come on then, which one of you greasy haired wankers want a bit of London punk!"

Lucy jumped from her seat. "Right then, I'm a police officer. I want you all to step back and calm down!"

"Fuck off plod!" shouted Tom.

"Yeah," shouted one of the Teds cockily, "fuck off back to Dock Green!"

Debbie moved forward and tried to help Dawn back to her feet. Dawn pushed her away. Debbie took out her handcuffs, pushed Dawn back down onto the ground, leant her knee onto her back firmly, grabbed one arm, then the other and cuffed her. "You're under arrest for assaulting a police officer."

The cocky Ted grabbed his pint mug glass, still half full of lager, and threw it. It smashed on the table with a single piece careering off and slicing across Suzie's cheek. She gasped with pain and placed her hand over the blood gushing from her face.

Rick picked up a chair and charged into the standing Teds, sending most of them to the floor. Lucy attempted to grab his arm but was thrown to the ground. The other punks ran across screaming, kicking and throwing punches. Debbie had laid across her prisoner. She was not letting her loose.

Lucy was back on her feet and grabbed Tom by his spikey hair. She pulled him down hard to the ground and after a brief wrestle had him cuffed.

The pub doors flew open and Bob, Danny, Fatboy and the rest of the task force raced in. Bob waded through bodies, pulling, pushing and shoving the fighting youths apart. Two of the lads were beaten and weary and sent sprawling to the floor. Fatboy ushered those clearly not wanting to fight over by the bar. Rick was still lashing out, the steel chain connected with a Ted's mouth. The cracking of teeth sent a shock wave down his fingers. A shot of joy and hatred pumped in his stomach at the same time. The lad fell forward trying clumsily to make a grab at Rick. Another well connected shot and the lad collapsed, motionless, to the ground.

Rick looked around him, he could see the fight was almost over and the police were rounding both Teds and Punks up. He sent one last kick into the Ted's face. All he could see was a pool of blood, ripped flesh and broken teeth. Rick bolted towards, the door shouting, "Run, Run!"

Outside he ran back down the road towards where he knew the car was parked. He felt for his pocket as he ran. The car keys were still there. Turning briefly, he saw that both Lucy and Debbie were racing up behind him.

"Stop! Police, Police!" commanded Lucy.

Rick stopped at the car and reached desperately into his pocket for the car keys. As he pulled them out they fell to the floor. Lucy and Debbie had caught up and stood either side of Rick.

Rick looked the woman police officers. He hated the police, but these were women. He didn't want to smash their faces, bash them up or kick their bodies into submission.

Lucy leant forward. Placing her hands on her knees she gasped for breath. She looked up at Rick. He looked clumsy and awkward, almost intimidated for all his toughness. She walked forward slowly and calmly. "Okay, it's all over now. I know you don't want to fight us. Just drop your hands down and lets just call this a day now."

Rick sighed hard, he knew the game was up. The adrenaline had stopped pumping and the seriousness of what he had done began to sink in. He turned towards the car and placed his hands behind his back. Lucy took his right arm and Debbie his left. Rick was cuffed and under arrest. A police van had arrived back at The Kings Arms and the battling youths were then taken into custody. Fatboy immediately left the pub and raced up the road to offer Lucy and Debbie back up. He arrived and saw that it was all under control.

"Bloody hell Lucy, that's amazing! Well done, bloody well done!" he smiled.

"Not me, it was Debbie who did most of the work," said Lucy bluntly.

Debbie beamed.

Fatboy stepped forward and shook her hand. "Well done Debbie, I'm Alan," he said with a big sloppy grin.

Lucy smiled, winked and shook her head knowingly. The police van arrived, and Rick was bundled away.

When Lucy wrote her report back at the nick she made sure that WPC Debbie Faulkner's part in the brawl was amplified. She could almost visualise Superintendent Luscombe's smile as he flicked through the pages. Debbie, in time, would make one hell of a police officer.

Chapter 22

"Thank you for agreeing to meet me for dinner Lucy," said Bob smiling. "It's been a while since I've been out for a curry, and besides, I thought it would be a good opportunity for us talk before you go back to Exeter."

"Sure," said Lucy. "It's nice to see Fatboy has been taking Debbie out."

"Yeah, they make a good couple. He's actually asked us to call him Alan now. Of course, Danny was first to start the Fatboy bit," he laughed.

"Fatboy, I mean Alan is a nice guy and Debbie could be the making of him."

"What about Danny, will he still be out on the prowl when he gets back, you know, just bedding anything with a pulse?" Bob said grinning.

"Danny's on a journey and sooner or later he'll find himself again," Lucy said fairly. "That may or may not be a good woman. But he will get there eventually, of that I'm sure."

"So, what are your plans when you get to Exeter?" asked Bob, pouring red wine into both their glasses.

"It's onwards and upwards. I think there's still a lot for me to learn and plenty of scope left to build on my career in the force. What about you Bob?"

"It'll be more of the same. I'll still be nicking criminals but as for private life I now know that I need to make changes."

"You mean Mary?"

"Yeah, as soon as I go back I'm going to tell her it's all over and wish her well."

"Are you sure that's what you want?"

"Yeah, definitely Lucy. These last months have made me really sit back and take stock of where I am and what I want."

"That's a good thing, right?"

"Well it is, sort of."

"Sort of?"

"Look Lucy we've become good friends right, you know really good friends and stuff."

"Yeah course, were mates Bob."

"Well I think of you as more than a friend Lucy."

There was a few second's silence as Lucy took a sip of wine.

"I find myself thinking about you constantly, first thing in the morning, during the day and last thing at night."

"Bob, stop. You're embarrassing me."

"I can't Lucy, I have to tell you how I feel. There are times when I just have this yearning feeling, it's almost uncontrollable. This overwhelming need to be near you, see you or hear your voice."

"Bob, I'm flattered, and I like you, but I've not encouraged any of this."

"I know that Lucy. I just find myself thinking how am I going to live after we all leave Newquay and go our separate ways. How do I wake up in the morning knowing that I'm not going to see you? I can't imagine what kind of life that would be. Feeling lost, not able to function without Lucy Penfold in my life."

"Bob, look I'm really sorry and I didn't see anything quite like this coming, I really didn't."

"Do you not feel anything for me Lucy?"

"Of course, I do, you're my friend, my colleague, a person who I trust and enjoy working with."

"And that's it, I'm just another officer passing through Lucy Penfold's career."

"I'm not sure what else you want me to say Bob. I can't lie about how I feel. It wouldn't be right and can't possibly help you or me."

"Is there someone else, somebody you've not mentioned Lucy because I can wait. I can be patient and wait if I know at some point we'd be together."

"There's no one else." Lucy took a deep breath and sighed. "I can never love you the way you want Bob."

Bob became visibly choked. Lucy could see tears collecting in his eyes.

"Bob don't get upset, that can't change the way that I feel. I can't love any man the way they'd want."

"You're cold Lucy, I'm pouring my heart out here."

"Bob we can talk all night and go over and over this, but it won't change the way that I feel." Lucy paused, nodded and said slowly, "I'm just not attracted to men. I like women Bob. I'm a lesbian."

Bob's chin fell open in shocked disbelief. "'Are you sure?"

Lucy laughed. "Of course I'm sure Bob. That doesn't mean I've met someone yet but when I do it won't be a man of that I'm sure."

"I didn't see that coming. I have just been blinded with my love for you." He shook his head and reached for his glass.

"Let's get this straight, if you can excuse the pun." They both laughed a little. "I like you Bob, you're my good friend. I like, care, trust and respect you and do not want to lose you as my friend. Do you understand that? Can we get through this and stay friends?"

"Yeah, yeah course we can. It's just that I've played tonight out in my head so many times and not once did it end like this. Invariably it ended up with you declaring your love for me and we'd marry, have children. You know, the whole nine yards."

"Out there Bob is a wonderful lady who will make you happy beyond your wildest dreams."

"I like that," he said raising his glass. "To good friends and future full of happiness."

"Cheers."

Two days later Lucy said good bye to Superintendent Luscombe and vowed to stay in touch with Bob. Her time at Newquay was over and she returned to Exeter.

Chapter 23

Lucy was called into Inspector Jessica Jones's office. She was pleased to be back in Exeter and around her friend and mentor.

"Well done Sprog. I've been reading through the reports. It looks as though Newquay was a big success for you and the task force."

"Yes Ma'am."

"Sprog, three hundred and thirty six arrests over a six month period is quite something and you seem to have won over Superintendent Luscombe. I'm not sure I've ever seen such a glowing report," she smiled. "All that said you and Bob will have to travel back tomorrow. There appears to be an outstanding warrant and two prisoners will need to be collected and returned Yorkshire. I'm sure I don't have to tell you this but any officer who loses a prisoner may as well go and join the Foreign Legion."

"Don't worry Ma'am we won't let them get away."

"I don't doubt that Sprog. Go on then, on your way."

"Thank you, Ma'am," said Lucy getting up to leave.

"Sprog."

"Yes Ma'am?"

"It's good to have you back."

Lucy beamed.

In the canteen she saw her friend Sergeant Pauline Pearson. "Hello Lucy, great to have you back."

"It's good to be back, thanks."

"How are things?"

"You mean?" asked Lucy smiling.

"No," laughed Pauline, "I mean in general."

"Everything's good really. I mean it would nice to meet someone. I think I'm ready for that now, but more pressing is my relationship with my mother."

"How do you mean?" asked Pauline leaning forward and resting her chin into her hand.

"Well things have never really been right, and I don't want to go into details, but I would just like it to be, well you know, better."

"Lucy, my love, mother and daughter relationships can be pretty complex and diverse. I know some who are best friends, others who talk on the phone once a week and some who live on opposite sides of the country. I'm not going to pry about your private business, but I would say that there are ups and downs no matter how positive or prickly the relationship. Most daughters, and I'm one of them, think that their mothers are overly critical and demanding. I think from a mother's perspective, and again this would be mine, that their daughters don't listen to them, that we make poor choices and have no time for them."

Lucy nodded.

"I think the first thing Lucy is to make the first move. I'm sure you've given this plenty of thought but think about how you feel in the relationship and what you can do to change."

"I have been calling Mother weekly and it does feel easier. In fact, she did come down to Newquay, albeit to leave the dog because she was away on holiday but, she did bring me down a Jubilee flag."

"See, now that tells me that your mum recognises something's wrong and in her own way is reaching out. Now how most people would look on ways to improve relationships is for the other person to change their ways."

"That would be nice and would certainly make it easier," said Lucy.

"But Lucy, you are not chained to your mother's actions. You are a strong independent woman who has the strength and ability to change your own reactions and responses. For what it's worth think that both mothers and daughters often have unrealistic expectations about their relationship. I mean we both, as kids, believed that our mums should be nurturing and always present. The great things is that it's never too late to alter your relationship."

"I've never really thought about like that. I mean Mother would say something and I'd fall straight into a mindset which gave a response which inevitably led to either a silence or an argument."

"Communication is probably the biggest problem for all us mother and daughters. I know that I believed that just because she was my mum that she should instinctively know how or what I was feeling. Now this is the strangest part. Having spoken at length with my mum, she felt pretty much the same. That as her daughter I should just know, and I must hold my hand up here Lucy and tell you that

I've spoken to my mum in a manner that I'd dare not speak to anyone else. It could get loud, abrupt and quite harsh at times. With time and talking in a controlled understanding way I found that communicating what was on my mind in a heartfelt and gentle manner we got over the issues. If I felt that mum was treating me like a child, then I'd say so but not in aggressive way. Just a simple you're not treating me like an adult mum."

"I'm not sure Mother and I have ever really done that."

"I truly believe that we have to be active listeners. You know, reflect on what is being said rather than just assuming. Lucy, I went on for years assuming my mum felt this or believed that. None of it was true and I built up a resistance in my own mind over, well nothing. These days I make sure I capture all that is being said because sometimes there can be an underlying message and that is what is truly being said. There were times when I felt that mum was being critical and didn't like me but what she truly meant was that she felt very protective of me because I wasn't protecting myself."

"I thought I was the only one. It's so good to hear that I'm not alone."

"You're not Lucy, far from it. I think, from what I've learnt, that to sustain a strong and healthy relationship you need to repair the damage quickly. That doesn't mean that you avoid conflict because, well that can be inevitable. However once done it should be resolved quickly and dealt with head on. When you don't resolve problems, it can result in all sorts of issues."

"How do you mean?"

"Well I could let it interfere with my own relationship. I could carry all sorts of baggage and dump it on someone I love. What I would say is that working it out with your mum, finding common ground for you both to grow and prosper on will probably be the best gift you could give to both yourself and your mum. You don't have to compromise and be unhappy. By all means pick your battles but if it's not that important then rather than it be an emotional tug of war just drop the rope. Let it go. Try to think of your mum with her own wounds and hurts. Our mums are probably the same age, they were raised and brought up in a different generation with different values and maybe difficult family relationships and issues. What I did was approach my mum's feelings with empathy and offered a compromise. So, knowing that she really wanted to meet up instead of saying stop asking me and I'm busy and that I turned around and said I'd would love to meet up with you mum, but my shifts don't allow it so can we do it next week?"

"How did she take that?"

Pauline smiled. "It worked perfectly. I can still convey the same message but with a little more thought and that has helped change my relationship with my mum. It's not perfect but it's pretty damn close now."

Lucy took a sip from her tea.

"You have to forgive your mum Lucy."

"That's a tough one Pauline. I do try but memories and the pain attached to them flood back sometimes."

"I can understand that but forgiving someone isn't saying that what they did was okay. It's not condoning, pardoning or minimizing the impact on you and your life. I see it as a key for well-being. I truly believe that you will need to forgive your mum to be healthy. The power of forgiveness Lucy is really for the person who forgives."

"Thank you, Pauline. You've given me plenty to think about. I'm going to have a good think about how I can do this."

"It can be difficult for us daughters to build our own identities. For a long while I believed that cutting my mum off was the only way I'd become my own person. I found that you can find your own voice and identity within the relationship. I've learnt how to deal with conflict and the negative emotions but what you cannot do is grow, develop and become your own person void of relationships. It's a balance of connection and separateness."

"I'm not sure how much my mother and I agree on. Not a lot probably," sighed Lucy.

"Then agree to disagree. You don't have to convince your mum to change her mind on something. I've learnt that mums can feel threatened or rejected when their daughters are making different decisions to ones that they would have made. It's then that you start believing that your mum disapproves of you and I'd become defensive. Mum and I still have major disagreements on certain issues but that's okay. I don't take it personally. Mum and I can still be close but neither of us have to change our opinions to please the other. The last thing I'd say Lucy, and this is important. You really must stick to the present. It will do no good going over old stuff from the past or it'll get the same old response. I'm sure you would but avoid sarcasm or facetiousness. It can easily be misinterpreted, causes hurt and will only take you one step further away from solving your relationship. You must set boundaries Lucy. That can be something simple like staying at a hotel or something when you go back home. If not that then when you're chatting on the phone and feel like the conversation is slipping away, then be clear and assert yourself by saying something like I really want to talk to you and keep our relationship going but if you start calling me names or criticise me then I'll have to hang up because it's just healthy for me. In my own opinion Lucy, I find setting boundaries in all relationships to be healthy and sustainable."

"Thank you, Pauline. You're a good friend."

Later that night Lucy called her mother.

***

Lucy met Bob at the train station. They travelled down to Newquay together. They were tasked with escorting two prisoners back to Yorkshire along with the stolen property; two six foot surf boards. Sadly, Superintendent Luscombe was not at the station, so they handcuffed the prisoners and placed the keys in their far side pockets, rolled their sleeves down so that members of the public would not see the cuffs and left for the train station. The prisoners were tasked with carrying the surf boards. As they walked across the station Lucy's prisoner bumped into a passing lady who wore a white jacket. It left a dark stain. The prisoner laughed and said, "Oh well, who cares?"

Lucy yanked on his cuffs.

"Oi that's police brutality that is."

"Just watch where you're going!" retorted Lucy.

"I've heard all sorts of stories about you lot. Most of you are more bent than the criminals."

"Really," sighed Lucy.

"Yeah really. Why do you think that people call you lot The Filth? I'll tell you. It's because some of your lot are out of control. They're more interested in getting a conviction than capturing who really committed the crime so they fit up innocent people and have them shipped off to prison. Mothers and children are separated from their loved ones. Then the poor bastards come out with a prison record and can't get a job, the family goes hungry and eventually breaks down and the route course is some overly ambitious copper who just wants to clear up crime."

"Quite the philosopher, aren't we?"

"It's not philosophical, it's a fact. The police force, up and down the country is riddled with corruption. Those at the top have allowed dishonesty and malpractice to flourish. You have Freemasons scratching each other's backs and now there's Operation Countryman. Yeah that's right I know about it, just about every working-class bod in the country knows about it. One of your own supergrasses has come forward and spilt the beans. Its common knowledge that some Old Bill have been arresting drug dealers and then going out and dealing cannabis, heroin, cocaine and amphetamines. What really makes me sick is the way they abuse their power for sexual gratification. Yeah that's right your fellow police officers are bullying or cajoling suspects, witnesses and even victims into having sex with them."

"You seem to know a lot about this."

"No, it seems you know very little about the people you work with."

"Well, I'm sure that Operation Countryman will seek out the law breakers and bring them to justice," said Lucy.

"You're just naive. As much as I'd like to see that happen it won't. The bent coppers will get pensioned off, others will be shipped off into the provinces, and you may see, after years of investigation and public cost, a few scapegoats. Then all the findings will be whisked off and classified secret because the establishment will become embarrassed by just how big this thing is. You'd probably be surprised if I told you that Old Bill in London have taken money from known criminals to lose evidence and then even take a percentage from robberies."

"So, how would you know something like that?"

"I did a few months in The Scrubs, that's Wormwood Scrubs in South London, for a minor possession charge. I talked and listened to a lot of my fellow inmates. Some of them were scum and deserved all they got. Others were interesting career criminals who played the game. If they were caught fair and square by good policing, then they held up their hands but then the palm was held out to make being a criminal easier providing you maintain the payments. The thin blue line between them and us was clouded until The Filth were just seen as untrustworthy, corrupt. If things had been allowed to continue I believe that you'd have seen Old Bill being taken out from around the country as fair game. Let's face it you could bribe the next one and you're off again."

"Well you'll have plenty to think about when you go down for theft," said Lucy sternly. "Now get on the train!"

The prisoners boarded the train and sat opposite each other. Bob and Lucy spoke very little. As Bob lit his cigarette Lucy's prisoner spoke. "I need to use the toilet."

"You'll have to hold it," said Lucy.

"I can't hold it, I'll piss myself. I'd like the toilet, please!" Lucy stood up and motioned the prisoner to follow. "You can't take me."

"Why not?"

"Because you'll see my cock."

Bob placed his hand over his mouth and laughed silently.

"I'll be fine," said Lucy rolling her eyes, "just don't ask me to touch it. Besides I've seen plenty and I'm sure they would have been mostly bigger."

The prisoner huffed as Bob sniggered.

Lucy and Bob delivered the prisoners without further incident. They were tired but decided to celebrate the assignment with a few drinks at a club and didn't get back to the hotel until gone 4am.

Chapter 24

Saturday August 19th, 1978: Devon and Cornwall Constabulary mounted the largest operation in their history following the disappearance of thirteen year old schoolgirl Genette Tate, from Aylesbeare Devon. Her bicycle was left in a rural area near Exeter Airport. Newspapers were found scattered around the lane only minutes after she had been speaking with two friends.

All available resources were activated in the search. Officers were rushed to Aylesbeare. A RAF helicopter had been called to help with the growing investigation. In the coming weeks RAF reconnaissance aircraft equipped with the latest aerial photography equipment were deployed, mounted officers from neighbouring counties Avon and Somerset and police dogs specially trained to sniff out human remains joined the search.

The Force's sub aqua unit mounted a painstaking operation to explore the three hundred and eighty-seven gravel pits, ponds, wells and stream in the area. Hundreds of farm buildings, ricks and silage pits were thoroughly searched, and acres of undergrowth cleared as the hunt widened.

As the hunt for Genette Tate, led by Detective Phillip Francis Diss continued, the village hall was turned into an incident room and for next six weeks more than eighty officers combed the fields and woodland within a five mile radius of the village. They were joined by the Marines and on one Saturday afternoon more than seven thousand members of the public came forward to help search nearby Woodbury Common.

The officers acted on every lead including letters and reports from over five hundred psychics and mediums. On the morning of Genette's disappearance there were several UFO reports.

For many months Genette's disappearance attracted significant local and national publicity. Her body had still not been found.

Chapter 25

"What are you drinking Lucy?"

"I'll have a whisky and ginger ale please," said Lucy

smiling.

Bob motioned the barman to bring two more drinks. "You know I'm still crazy about you," joked Bob. "Yeah course you are," she said raising her eyebrow.

"Here Bob," said an officer Lucy hadn't seen before, "did you hear about Sergeant Hoggins?"

"Nah, what's that all about then?"

"Well some people just fall straight out of a top story window into a flower bed, don't they?"

"What do you mean?"

"Well you know what old Hoggins is like, don't you? I mean, I've seen three-legged race horses with more get up and go than him."

"So, what then?" asked Bob shrugging his shoulders.

"Well he's out and about and a call comes in to attend a house fire. So, old Hoggins has taken a leisurely drive over to check it out. I swear he's only been treading water until retirement. Anyway, he's got out the car and this guy has come running out the building coughing and spluttering. So Hoggins has taken off his jacket and started to go in when this bloke has told him not to bother because there was no-one in there. Well for some reason, only known by old Hoggins, he's just gone in anyway. I mean he's walking around with smoke and flames everywhere. Well he's stumbled into this room and sees a woman on the floor. He's gone to pick her up and she has been beaten senseless. There was blood and claret everywhere. As he's helped her up she's gasping please, my children, please save my children they're upstairs. So Hoggins has all but turned into superman and dragged her to the doorway and then raced up the stairs. He's grabbed the two children from the burning room. They were hiding under the bed crying. He's brought them all outside and then gone and nicked the father. It turns out the bastard has beaten his wife and then set fire to the place to get rid of them all. Well he ended up being awarded a Chief Constable's Commendation."

"Sounds like a hero to me," said Lucy angrily.

"Nah you don't know him sweetheart. The bloke was a right knob, no one liked him!"

Lucy stood up and leant forward. Through a clenched grin she said "Yes, I do know him and he's my Sergeant. I suggest you say what you have to say to his face and stop running around tittle tattling like a bloody washer woman up on the Burnt Road Estate."

"Wow, you're touchy," he laughed nervously.

"Catch you later mate, "said Bob motioning him to leave.

Inspector Jessica Jones stood at the bar doorway and waved Lucy towards her.

"Sprog, I've got something I'd like you to do. It'll be good experience," she said handing Lucy a note. "The address is on there. It's only a small station but frankly it needs sorting and I think your enthusiasm is just what the place needs right now. You leave in the morning. Accommodation has been organised."

"How long is the assignment Ma'am?"

"Till I say so. Now off you go and get ready."

***

Lucy stood outside the police station and took a deep breath. This was so much smaller than she had been used to. It could have been a 1930s converted house. Portishead was just a small town but if Jessica Jones thought she'd gain something from it then she'd concluded she'd just suck it up and throw herself into the task at hand.

"Good morning, I'm WPC Lucy Penfold. I think you're expecting me."

"Yes HI, I'm constable Craig Towers. We heard that you were coming in from Exeter."

They both turned as a door slammed and a uniformed figure raced across to a waiting suspect.

SMACK!

The officer slapped the suspect hard across the head. He held up both his arms to protect his face. The officer smacked him again and then again. Silence fell in the station.

"You're a low life piece of shit. The kind of thing decent people find on their shoes after a brisk walk through the park. Now I know you nicked it, you know you nicked in fact every fucking person in Portishead knows you bloody nicked it. So, stop," he smacked the suspect hard around the head again, "wasting our time with your pointless denials and worthless alibis."

The suspect rubbed his head frantically. "Please, Constable Knight, it wasn't me. I was home with my mum."

Constable Knight drew his open hand back as if ready to deliver another hard slap. Suddenly he stopped, let his arm down and smiled menacingly. "Okay," he said lowering his voice to an almost hiss then lighting two cigarettes and handing one to the suspect, "just toddle off with the Constable and sign your confession and we'll say no more about it. I mean we really don't want to be dragging your poor old mum down here in her wheelchair for hours and hours quizzing her about you and your ware bouts, do we?" He nodded to an officer who led the suspect into the interview room.

Lucy looked on in shocked disbelief.

Constable Trevor Knight was a tall, overweight man in his late forties. He was grey and balding with steely, blue eyes. He had the look of a once handsome man, though his features were marred by his surly and aggressive expression.

Constable Knight looked at his watch and went towards the door.

"Right I have people to see and places to go. I'll be back in a couple of hours if anyone needs me." He glanced at Lucy dismissively and strode out of the station with the arrogance of an officer way beyond his rank.

"Who the hell was that?" asked Lucy in sheer amazement.

"Congratulations you've just met Constable Trevor Knight although he's better known as The Butcher."

"The Butcher?"

"Oh yes, I could tell you stories you simply wouldn't believe. This, WPC Penfold will be a baptism of fire. The Butcher runs this place with a rod of iron. No one crosses him, and I do mean no one so watch yourself. Keep your thoughts and opinions to yourself. You really don't want to make an enemy of The Butcher. Believe me."

Craig led her through to the small canteen and poured her a cup of tea.

"How long have you been here Craig?" asked Lucy taking short sip of the hot drink.

"Too long, I should have moved from here years ago."

"Why haven't you? What I've just seen is awful. I've seen some things but that is the worst by far."

"That Lucy was nothing, a mild start to the day. You wait until he's really angry. Suspect, member of the public, fellow officer. He doesn't care, his eyes glaze over and then that's it."

"What you mean he gets physical?"

"If by physical you mean smacks in the face, kick in the nuts or head butted so a nose bleed. Yeah, that's The Butcher. I've seen him tear down the biggest of guys here. You could say he's very territorial and this station and the town is his domain. I mean the man has twenty-five years in, and all here."

"I don't understand why somebody hasn't blown the whistle, you know just told someone."

"The Butcher runs it all and that means the senior officers here. They turn a blind eye. They don't want to argue with him, they live in the town for Christ's sake and besides he cleans up just about every crime."

"By that you mean he intimidates and bullies suspects into confessions?"

Craig shrugged his shoulders.

"Craig you're a smart man and you clearly don't sign up to this. Why haven't you said something?"

"Lucy when I first got here I got on fine with The Butcher and then bit by bit he just changed towards me. He tries to control people rather than inspire. He lacks any empathy. I've seen him beat a suspect to a pulp and strike an officer in the middle of the station in front of everyone. A nasty piece of work. Having just called out one officer for being a homosexual, he told him that he should be wearing a pink uniform with feathers. That he was a disgusting poof that hung around outside men's toilets. One day without any provocation he grabbed the officer by the throat and lifted him clean off the floor. He held him while the officer choked and pleaded to be let go but The Butcher just spat out one insult after another. When he finally let him down he turned to the rest of us and said calmly that if that poof didn't look so queer he wouldn't have had to hit him."

"That's unbelievable. What happened to the officer?"

"He left the force. It was a real shame because he was well liked by everyone. Whatever his sexual orientation was it really had nothing to do with his ability to be a damn good copper."

"Where's Constable Knight off to now then? It sounded a bit ominous, people to see and places to go."

"Oh, its 11am. He'll be at Ruby's."

"Ruby's?"

"Yeah, Ruby is the local brass, you know on the game, a prostitute."

"Yes, I know what a brass is Craig," said Lucy rolling her eyes.

"Sorry of course you do. Well every other day, about 11am, he'll disappear over to Ruby's and do whatever he does."

"I'm stunned. I have never come across this kind of behaviour before and believe me I have seen some things."

"Drink up and I'll show you where your living quarters are. I think you're due out on car patrol tomorrow. Don't forget just keep your head down and don't do anything to annoy him. If you need anything then just give me a shout."

"Well," thought Lucy, "Jessica has certainly given me a challenge here. This is a bloody nightmare!"

***

The following morning Lucy was up and ready. She stopped by the canteen where she poured herself and Craig a cup of tea then introduced herself to her colleagues. They all seemed friendly enough. Constable Trevor Knight, The Butcher, entered the room. It became silent, Lucy could feel the menace.

"Right, so we have a new split arse in the station then." He looked around the room and then focused in on Lucy. "Well come on then WPC Penfold, grab your make-up and let's get off."

Lucy swallowed the retort she was dying to give. This wasn't the time. Her strategy would be to observe, listen, take notes and decide how she'd handle this Neanderthal when the time came.

The Butcher stopped by the police Panda car and faced Lucy with a stern frown.

"Let's be clear, I'm driving and for the record I always drive. You will have heard about me by now and I suspect that most of it is true. So, don't piss me off," he said slamming both his hands down hard on the Panda car's roof, "and we'll get on like a house on fire."

Lucy nodded, she felt deeply uncomfortable. This was no veiled threat but a clear warning.

The Butcher drove down into the town and stopped outside the local café on a yellow line.

"First things first. I always start my day with a good breakfast. That is the cornerstone for every good crime fighting copper so we're in here Cosy Café."

They both entered the café. It was half full and seemed quite vibrant until they saw The Butcher.

"Good morning Archie. I've got a new split arse with me today. Just showing her the ropes, you know how it is. Anyway, I'm proper hungry so I want your mega breakfast with an extra egg and two extra sausages alright. Oh, and two cups of tea."

Archie sighed and nodded. "What can I get for you?" he asked pouring the tea pot.

"Hello Archie, I'm Lucy and just a couple rounds of toast with marmalade will be fine thank you."

Archie looked up and smiled. "Take a seat Lucy and I'll bring it over."

The Butcher scooped up his breakfast with sliced bread and shovelled it into his mouth without looking up and only pausing to take a sip from the tea. Lucy sat in silence. He took the last slice of bread and ran it around the plate scooping up the baked bean sauce and egg. Swallowing hard he reached into his pocket and took out a box of Rothman cigarettes. He lit one and inhaled the smoke deep into his lungs and then looked skywards as he exhaled.

"You finished then?"

"Yes, thank you I'm all done," answered Lucy her face sneering down.

"Well come on then, we ain't got all day," he joked.

Lucy left the table and asked Archie how much she owed. "Nah, that's alright. I like to do my bit," he said tensing up.

"That's very good of you Archie but I insist. I always pay my way thank you."

"Oh, okay. Well that'll be sixty pence please," he smiled.

The Butcher rose from the table, stubbed out his cigarette and walked towards the door.

"What about PC Knight? How much was his please?"

"No, that's okay. We have an arrangement and I'm very happy," Archie's voice trembled full of fear.

"What you mean he doesn't pay?" Archie shook his head.

"Has he ever paid?"

"I don't want any trouble," he said shrugging his shoulders. Lucy nodded, smiled and left.

The Butcher was sat in the police car. He hooted twice and gestured her over furiously.

An old man walked past with his golden Labrador. The dog stopped, sniffed the lamppost and then squatted down passing two logs. The man looked away and then tugged on the dog's lead. As he started to walk away The Butcher leapt out the car.

"Oi you!" he called.

"Who me?" said the old man.

"Yes you. What do you think your game is?"

"I'm sorry officer, I don't know what you mean," he said now looking increasingly concerned.

"Your dog has taken a bloody great shit on the pavement and you are just walking off. What do you think there are people following dog owners around just waiting to clear up after their dogs?"

"No, I'm sorry. I just didn't think."

"No, you didn't bloody think. You were happy to just walk off leaving a bloody great steaming turd on the ground for someone else to either walk in or clear up. That sir is unacceptable. So how are you going to remedy this?"

"I'll keep a closer eye on my dog and try to make sure he toilets in the park."

"Not good enough!"

"I'm not sure what else I can do other than apologise and make sure it doesn't happen again."

"Pick it up!" "What?"

"You heard me fine. There's a bin over there," he said pointing towards a steel dustbin by the side of alleyway. "Pick it up and put it in the bin."

The old man gave a nervous laugh. "Surely you're joking with me officer?"

"No, I'm not. You are responsible for the shit your dog left on the pavement. Pick it and put it into the bin."

The old man reached into his pockets and shrugging his shoulders he said, "I don't have a hankie or toilet paper."

"You've got hands that work don't you. So, pick it up and put it the bin."

"Officer, please," he pleaded, "I'm an old man and I'm truly sorry but I can't pick up dog shit."

"But you expect others to or worse still walk in it and have dog shit on their shoes all day. Get it picked up now! I do not have all day and right now you're really trying my patience."

"No, I'm not picking it up," the man said, feigning courage.

The Butcher took several steps towards him. His demeanour became even more menacing. The old man cowered and shrunk before him.

"Okay, okay I'll do it," he said apologetically.

The Butcher continued his glare until the both logs had been picked up and placed in the dustbin.

"Okay, now get on your way and don't let me ever see your dog shit on the streets again or I'll have it taken away and put down. Do you understand me?"

"Yes sir," the old man answered in a low broken voice.

"I asked you if you understood me!" barked the Butcher!

"Yes sir, it won't happen again."

"Good, now on your way and get those hands cleaned up," he smirked.

Lucy was speechless.

The police car proceeded along the main road. The Butcher looked down at his watch and then drove into the Tesco Food Stores car park. A group of young teenage school girls, in uniform, stood together chatting. The Butcher pulled alongside them. He looked the blond girl up and down. She wore a short, pleated, red tartan skirt and knee-high white socks, a white blouse and a tie that hung loosely around her neck.

"Hello Julie, good to see you in your uniform," he paused for a few seconds, "and back at school."

Julie looked at her friends and then back at the Butcher. She nodded awkwardly.

The Butcher looked her up and down again smiling and then drove slowly past and parked up in a bay. He looked around the car park for a while and then said, "Here he is. Right Penfold, see that scruffy looking tramp over there?" he said pointing to a youngish man who was clearly living on the streets, "That's Sid and he's about to do his usual."

"His what?" asked Lucy.

"Any minute now he'll run through Tesco and try to grab a bottle of vodka."

They both stepped out of the car.

"On your way then, go and follow him," he laughed out loud.

Lucy walked towards Sid as he entered the building. She increased her pace. As she walked inside Sid looked over his shoulder and, giving a look of stark surprise, he turned and ran off. Lucy gave chase. Sid pushed through the shoppers and side stepped the trolleys with ease. Racing down the alcohol isle he grabbed a bottle of vodka and began unscrewing the lid. Lucy called repeatedly for him to stop but Sid ignored her and worked even faster. He threw the cap to the floor and began hungrily swallowing the vodka. He took deep gulps, with almost half a bottle now gone he looked back to see Lucy was gaining on him. An employee stood at the isle end with his arms outstretched as if ready to save a goal. Sid ran to the left and then quickly darted to the right. The employee lunged and missed him and fell into the stacked shelf. Lucy side stepped the employee and continued to race after Sid who was now guzzling the last of the bottle down. Sid dropped the empty bottle, it smashed into small pieces on the floor, then he ran through the shocked shoppers towards the exit. Just as he thought he was home free The Butcher stepped out and threw a hard punch straight into his stomach. Both his legs left the floor momentarily before he fell to his knees holding his stomach.

"You Sid, are nicked!"

The Butcher grabbed Sid's collar and began to drag him along the floor towards the police car. Lucy stopped behind him. She leaned forward to catch her breath.

"Sid does this shit all the time. This isn't the first time he's done it and I very much doubt it'll be his last. We'll have him picked up and stuck in a cell. He'll be pissed now but once he's sobered up he'll be processed."

The Butcher pulled out a cigarette, lit it and shook his head.

Lucy found herself biting her lip. Everything about this man was wrong.

***

Sid was taken away in a police van and The Butcher continued his patrol. A few hours passed by without incident. Lucy avoided asking open ended questions and small talk. She nodded occasionally and looked out the window giving the odd grunt as The Butcher told tales of his heroism.

They stopped the panda car outside a fish and chip shop in the High Street.

"You hungry?"

"No, I'm fine thanks."

"Oh, I know, on a diet are we?" he laughed.

"No, just not hungry. I'll eat later."

"Suit yourself."

The Butcher strode into the fish and chip shop, to the front of the queue and came back out again carrying a large white package in just minutes. He got back into the car and opened the package revealing a large cod, chips and a sausage in batter. The smell of heavily salted and vinegar food was overwhelming. It did make her feel a little hungry. Lucy was embarrassed and uncomfortable to be seen or associated with this man, her fellow officer. She would eat later alone in her quarters.

***

Back at the station Lucy made a cup of tea in the canteen. Craig came in, his face lit up.

"How was your day Lucy?" he asked.

"Well I made a right balls up earlier."

"How's that?" Craig said with a comforting tone.

"Well I saw this man staggering along the road and I called out quite innocently, did you have a good night sir, and he answered 'No I lost my bloody legs in Korea!' Craig I was hoping the ground would open up and swallow me."

"That would be old Bill Tennyson, he can be a bit of a grump at times but a lovely old fella on the whole. What about The Butcher, how did you get on?"

"What do you think?" asked Lucy pouring a second cup

"He can be a real nightmare Lucy. To be honest he scares the shit out of me and well…. Probably everyone in the station. When I was first posted here we were out on patrol and he'd drive by pubs that were clearly still open after hours and pay no attention to them, then pull into others and cause mayhem. I later learnt that he drank in those pubs he avoided when he was off duty."

"I bet he didn't pay either," Lucy hissed.

"Yeah, so you've seen that? He's been doing that for years. Breakfast, newspapers, chips, Chinese food you name it and he eats or drinks there and doesn't pay. The scary part of it all Lucy is that he doesn't think that anything he's doing is wrong."

***

The next day a burglary in progress was called into the station. Lucy and several officers were despatched to the scene. The Butcher led eight officers, excluding Lucy, to the back of the building. Lucy couldn't understand why both exits hadn't been covered. She stayed out of sight but with a clear view of the front door. She could hear them fumbling on the radio with no clear direction. The front door opened and a tall man carrying a large bag left the building. Lucy stepped into his path. The burglar dropped his bag and ran forwards. Lucy side stepped him as he passed, grabbed his arm and threw him clean over her hip. He crashed down onto the floor, winded and unable to move. Lucy took his wrists and placed handcuffs on him. She read him his rights and radioed her colleagues to say that she had arrested the offender and he was in her custody at the front of the building. The Butcher pushed through the dumbfounded officers and gabbed the burglar by the scruff on the neck and dragged him over to the car. He was bundled in and taken back to the nick.

Back at the station Lucy told the Sergeant that she had made the arrest.

"No, you didn't split arse, you weren't even there!" shouted The Butcher.

"While you and the Keystone cops were roaming aimlessly around the back of the building I made the arrest," said Lucy bluntly.

"Like fuck did you. This is my collar. I made this arrest and I did it on my own!"

"Are you living on another planet PC Knight, because so far everything I've seen from you is totally alien in a modern police force."

"You need to shut up and tow the fucking line. I'm the top dog around here and if I say jump all you need to ask is how high!"

Lucy shook her head as other officers began to gather around. All she could think about since she first arrived was the thin blue line comments made by the surfer she'd arrested and taken to Yorkshire with Bob.

"Really and you think that's the way to inspire others is it? To shout and bully your way around the station, the town, to officers and the public alike."

The Butcher clenched his fists and glared with menace.

"So that's it, you want to take a swing at me now?" asked Lucy

"If you were my fucking daughter I'd wipe the floor with you!" said The Butcher, his face white with rage now.

"Really, well bring it on. You're a PC with twenty-five years in and you walk around like you're a Chief Constable. You're not, you've failed. You've failed in your career, you've failed to inspire or motivate others, you've failed the town and you've failed to represent the law, but most of all you've failed YOURSELF!"

Lucy stood her ground her eyes firmly fixed on the Butcher. There was a clear sense of uneasiness in the room.

The Butcher clenched his fists over and over as Lucy's words sank in. He looked around at the officers who each in turn lowered their eyes. He was alone. The Butcher took a step forward. Lucy turned side on and raised her hands. She knew that The Butcher could clearly inflict significant damage, but Lucy refused to back down. The Butcher stopped, he looked around the room once again. Finally, he spun around and left the room. The tension in the room eased immediately. Lucy could hear whispered comments like 'I don't believe it' and 'bloody hell' around her. Lucy smiled to herself having held and reinforced the thin blue line.

***

The following day The Butcher didn't turn in for his shift. The rumour had spread around the station that he'd seen an Inspector and they'd agreed for him to retire early. Lucy went out on foot patrol, it was raining hard. She was covering herself as best she could when she spotted a car being pushed by a woman. Lucy crossed the road.

"Hello, having problems?"

"Yes," came a voice from inside the car, "the car won't start."

"Do you know what the problem is?" asked Lucy

"I think it's the battery. We left the lights on. My wife, love her heart, was trying to give me a push to bump start the car."

"Okay, get ready and we'll both give you a push," said Lucy smiling at the rain drenched wife.

Within a few yards the driver dropped the clutch and then bumped and started. He revved the engine and his wife ran out of the rain to the passenger side.

"Thank you, officer. I really appreciate your help."

He reached into his pocket and offered her two pounds.

"No, I'm sorry but I cannot take that. Besides I'm happy to help. But, if you truly are grateful the police station is just around the corner. There's a charity box in the reception for widows and orphans. Just pop it in there."

"Will do and thank you again," he said cheerily waving to her as he drove off.

The car drove away, and Lucy continued her patrol as the first burst of thunder brought further downpours.

Lucy returned to Exeter the following week.

Chapter 26

Lucy was told that because she had nice handwriting and a brain she would be joining the Murder Squad working in the office. She quickly found out that women were usually picked for this role, because stations were contacted around the force and asked to nominate officers for the position. It was a commonly held belief that women were expendable and the weakest link, and therefore clearly the best choice for an office bound position. The initial role involved little more than writing key parts of a statement onto a 5 x 7 post card, name, address and date of birth and then placing the card in a large circular filing system. This was a long way from the active policing Lucy had experienced previously.

Until the 1970s most of the UK's police forces had little or no experience in dealing with major enquiries. It was not unusual for Scotland Yard to be called in and provide assistance. The resource consisted of a superintendent and a sergeant. The superintendent would analyse the documentation and would control the enquiry by an index and action book known as Book 40.

Individual forces, over time, adapted the Metropolitan Police system to suit their own purposes as they carried out more and more major investigations. The original system became lost, which hindered assisting officers on other major enquiries as they did not understand the system. Following the high-profile lorry driver Peter Sutcliffe, dubbed the Yorkshire Ripper case, where he seriously assaulted twenty woman and killed thirteen of them, and ran from 1974–1981, the Home Office became concerned with the lack of standard operating procedures. The crimes were committed in seven different police force areas. The Ripper appeared in several enquiries but due to the lack of standard procedures his name wasn't highlighted as a potential offender.

The police force came under severe criticism and as result the government initiated an inquiry led by Lawrence Byford, HM Chief Inspector of Constabularies. In December 1984 his report was published leading to a standard manual of procedures.

In 1986 the Holmes, Home Office Large Major Enquiry System, specification was agreed, purchased and introduced to every British police force.

When the system arrived, many officers struggled with its introduction. The concept of one standardised system for every force in a single language had very clear advantages. If a murder took place with a hammer for example, it was possible to raise a series of actions including who was the manufacturer, who were the trade distributors and who and where the retail distributors were located. The police were now able to collate information

in one place, with standardised input by all operators. This meant that interrogation of the system was swift and accurate. Any persons who came into the system for more than one enquiry could be cross analysed by the computer and highlighted for the attention of the investigating officer from then on, unlike Peter Sutcliffe who entered the old hand written system on five occasions without detection.

Lucy was told that she would attend a course with ten groups of ten candidates for ten weeks on the new Holmes system. There would be a final examination that had an eighty per cent minimum pass rate and the course would be the most challenging known to any police officer to date. Those who did not pass the exam would never touch the computer again. Those who came first in each group would go on to complete another three week's intensive researcher course.

With seventy-five male and twenty-five female attendees the best performing top ten candidates were all woman. Lucy completed all her exams and tests including the researcher course.

Chapter 27

"Have you got time for a quick cuppa?" asked Bob with a big sloppy grin.

Lucy looked at her watch and shrugged her shoulders. "No, sorry, I'm being sent out on a call. I'll catch you for a drink in the bar later okay?"

"Sounds good, "winked Bob.

Lucy had been called out to an old derelict house in a corner of a quiet cul-de-sac in the country. She smiled noticing how splendid the views were from behind the wildly overgrown garden. The main path was missing with just the odd grey stained, broken paving slab. She pushed lightly against the rotten front door and it swung open exposing stacks of daily newspapers bound and stacked all through the house leaving just a small corridor to the front room. Lucy entered gingerly and followed the pathway.

"Hello, hello is any one at home?" There was no answer.

"Hello, I'm WPC Lucy Penfold. Is anyone at home?"

There was no answer.

As she pushed the door open and entered the room the smell of filth attacked her sinuses. Lucy saw a motionless male figure propped up in an arm chair, a dead body. His head had fallen forward. It looked as if he was wearing an oil skinned jacket. She could see through the jacket opening a length of rope used as a belt to hold up his trousers.

"Hello dearie." Lucy almost jumped out her skin as a very slight, old wrinkly woman with a mop of grey hair touched her shoulder.

"I'm sorry dearie, I didn't mean to startle you."

Lucy shook her head. "No, that's fine. I'm sorry, I did call out, but no one answered."

"That's okay dearie, I'm a little hard of hearing. Would you like a nice cup of tea?"

Lucy took a short look around the room.

"No thank, but maybe later. Can you tell me what happened?"

The old woman went on to tell Lucy how she came down after a night's sleep only to find Max, her husband, dead in the chair. Lucy went back out to the police car and called in for a doctor. Within twenty minutes the doctor had arrived and certified the death.

Lucy took a walk around the room and spotted a large, neat, pile of match boxes of the sideboard. She picked the first and it had written in clear capital letter: NOSE PICKINGS JUNE 1955 – JULY 1968. She placed it back and picked up another: TOE NAIL CLIPPINGS MAY 1968 – DECEMBER 1974. There were others reading: HAND NAIL CLIPPINGS, BELLY BUTTON PICKINGS and EAR WAX all dated. Lucy placed them on the side, shook her hands and rubbed them down her skirt.

The widow came back in carrying a garment. "Please don't let him go without his best jumper."

Lucy had been asked to travel with the body to the mortuary. She watched as they labelled the body, made a statement and then called the undertakers.

The dead man's clothes were saturated in an oil like substance. At first Lucy had thought that had been the design. It wasn't, each of his garments were soaked in a thick clear liquid. The undertaker arrived and refused to go through the pockets.

Lucy grabbed a pair of rubber gloves and pushed pass them and began to carry out the search. She placed a front door key, a black, rubber sink plug and a cigarette butt on the table. She then leant across the body and reached into his back pocket. Lucy placed an object down the table, the undertaker let out a minor gasp as she unwrapped a white five-pound note from the 1950s.

The body was then taken to a shower room and hosed down before being placed in a drawer.

Lucy couldn't help to think, "Is that it, is that all we become at the end?"

The thought quickly passed when she got back in the car. The radio reported an accident just a few miles from her location, so she buckled up and raced off to the scene. As she drove out onto the High Street she could see several cars backed up. Lucy parked, placed her hat firmly on her head and strode towards the accident. A male officer had begun to wave the traffic on while another moved on-lookers.

"What happened here?" asked Lucy.

"So far, we have reports of a stray dog, possibly a sandy coloured Labrador, that was seen running between the cars. It ran out onto the main road causing the blue Ford Cortina to brake sharply, swerve and hit the White Ford Granada side on."

"Okay, thank you," said Lucy walking closer to the accident.

Lucy looked over the rear of the car and slowly walked around where she saw a woman slumped head down through the broken screen onto the bonnet. Looking over at a fellow officer who shook her head at a slow pace Lucy knew then that the woman had died.

"Have you got any gloves?"

"Sorry?"

"Gloves, you know gloves."

"Yeah sure," Lucy reached into her pocket and handed over her black leather gloves.

The officer, who was in plain clothes, put on the gloves. "Okay," she said, "I need you to lift the head please."

Lucy did as she was told. The officer began to remove particles of red blood-stained glass from the dead woman's face.

"Okay, that's it now. You can let her head back down, nice and easy."

The woman handed Lucy back her blood soiled gloves, turned and walked away.

Who the hell was that? thought Lucy.

***

Later that evening back at the station in the bar Lucy was enjoying a drink with Bob, Jim and Danny.

"So, what do you reckon then Lucy, am I looking good or what?" said Danny combing his hair in front of mirror.

"Danny mate," laughed Bob, "I've never seen you walk pass a mirror. You must love yourself."

"Bob, if you want to get laid then you have to take proper care of yourself."

"I think you look good Danny but," smiled Lucy, "I'm not so sure about that jacket."

"The jacket, this is pucker stuff straight out of Eden's Menswear, none of that C&A stuff old Bob wears. Oh, wait a minute. I'm not falling for that old stuff again Lucy."

"What stuff's that then"' asked Bob leaning forward.

Danny took a large sip from his glass and then lit a cigarette.

"Well when we were in Newquay I came downstairs, all done up to the nines ready to go out on the pull and I've asked Lucy how I looked. Anyway, I'm wearing a navy-blue suit with a grey shirt. I'm looking in the mirror and thinking 'I'm looking the dogs bollocks'. Well Lucy has said, yeah you look great, but don't you have a pink tie. So, I've gone yeah, no problem and raced off upstairs and put this pale pink tie. She's looked me up and down and gone don't you have another suit? Anyway, to cut a long story short I've gone back upstairs and put on a brown suit. When I came back down she's looked me up and down and said nah I think I liked what you were wearing when you first came down. She's a right bloody wind up that Lucy."

"That was such a laugh," said Lucy. "Newquay was quite the time."

"Well personally I think you put the mockers on the whole night after that wind up."

"Why's that then?" asked Bob.

"Well I've taken this lovely little sort out. You know the type: hello my name is Chloe and I have big boobs and a bottom. Not too much in the brain department but, a guaranteed shag."

"So, didn't she like your suit?"

"No, you Tinkerbell. I've taken her out for dinner. It was a nice restaurant. You know the kind a little bit upmarket. I thought it would be worth it. Anyway, I could see she had a bit of a cold, but I just ordered a nice bottle of wine thinking I'd set the scene and see if I could break my own record of three hours and in the sack banging like a shit house door in the wind."

"So, did you?" Bob took a deep breath.

"Well, I've poured her a nice glass of red and turned on the smooth bollocks and she's sneezed and I'm not kidding this fucking great bogey bubble has come out of her nose. Well she just jumped up fast and disappeared to the toilets with her hand over her face. Call me old fashioned but after that there was no way I was going to attempt the deed with her."

"What happened then?"

"When she got back to the table all red faced and that. I just made my excuses and fucked off to find something else."

"Was the whole night a right off then?"

"Well you wouldn't think so because I'd seen this lovely little blonde sort, recently divorced, called Sandra. You know the type

Bob, all fucked up man haters. So, I decided to not write the night off as a complete loss but try to salvage it with a second shag. I mean she did have this special way with her tongue."

"Alright Danny," said Lucy shaking her head, "spare us all the gory details."

"Anyway," Danny carried on ignoring Lucy, "I've slipped round there, and she's invited me in. She was dressed in all this gymnastics type stuff and said that she was working out in the living room. So, I've followed her in and even patted her bum which was met with a little giggle. Right now, I'm thinking that I'm definitely right in here. I sat down while she did all these exercises. Did you ever do handstands when you were at school she asked. Nah I've said but they're pretty cool. I stood up and she's held her hands above her head and told me to hold her legs as she rocked back and forth and then went right down. She was balancing on her hands, so I grabbed her legs and she has slipped out this horrible gut-wrenching fart straight in my face. I mean I could feel the wind brush up against my skin and the smell. Fuck me it was rancid. Like old boiled eggs left in a fridge with no electricity for a month."

"Urgh, that's horrible," Bob said putting his hand over his mouth. "What did you do?"

"All I could mate. I screamed out you dirty bitch, dropped her legs and walked out the front door. Nah the whole night was a write off after you played me up Lucy. I think you put the mockers on me."

"I kind of find the whole farting thing quite funny," said Jim who had been listening intently.

"Really," said Lucy with a look of disgust.'

"Sure, when I was a kid at school I use to really get off by farting in small enclosed spaces. You know slide up next to the teacher in the store room and as long as there are other kids in there I'd let out a right nasty silent but violent variety. I'd slip back and just wait to see when the smell hits and people's eyes start watering and then say out loud what was that and use a kid's name who was in there. Like, urgh Harry that's horrible, what did you say - now don't sniff it all up? The kid would go red and everyone would look at him as the perpetrator. Sometimes I'd even drop to the floor holding my throat and point at someone in complete disgust," he laughed out loud. "That one always worked a treat."

"That Jim, is just horrible," Lucy said with disdain.

"Yeah but funny."

"Probably not for the kid who got blamed."

"Those were nothing. One occasion I stood right next to this gorgeous, drop dead, woman. Just in front of her was this muscle-bound bloke in a T shirt with his biceps hanging out. Anyway, I'd brewed up this proper nasty one and just dropped it, waited a few seconds and backed off slowly. You should have seen their faces. The bloke looked her up and down like she was some kind of walking turd and she's just waving her hand frantically in front of her face. Guys I kid you not, I laughed all the way home."

"You Jim," said Bob scrunching his face up, "are one dirty bastard."

"Yeah, I always thought you were the nice one," said Lucy sipping from her glass.

"Me too," said Danny. "I used to look up at you as my kind of mentor. You know a beacon of all that is good and righteous in the world." He paused for a few seconds. "Either that or you're a thirty year old virgin who has to wank himself off five times a day because he can't get a woman."

"I get plenty of woman thank you Danny. I just don't parade them around," retorted Jim.

"What real ones or the blow-up kind you get from sex shops?"

"Okay this is getting nasty now, what are you all drinking?" asked Lucy nodding warily.

The guys gave her their orders and she went up to the bar. Someone brushed past. Lucy turned to look.

"Oh hello, I'm Pippa," she said holding out her hand, "we met at the accident earlier."j

Lucy stared at her, open mouthed. Pippa was the most stunning woman she had ever seen. She looked almost Spanish with her olive coloured skin and long, straight, black glossy hair. She had the most piercing grey eyes Lucy had ever encountered. They were mesmerising. She was stunningly beautiful, every pore from her smooth, curvaceous body oozed sex appeal. Lucy inhaled her perfume, it was Poison, her favourite. Pippa's voice was clear and precise like a presenter from the BBC.

"Hi, yes I'm Lucy, Lucy Penfold."

"I know that Lucy," she purred raising an eyebrow. "We must go out on a girlie night sometime."

"I'm sorry, but I'm busy thank you," Lucy replied nervously.

"Maybe another time," Pippa smiled maintaining constant eye contact then slowly turned and strutted towards the exit. Lucy's eyes followed her every movement. Her heart was thumping, her mouth went dry and her hands were sweating. Lucy found herself thinking how easy it would be to let Pippa slide so effortlessly into her life.

Chapter 28

Sometime had passed and Lucy still found herself thinking about Pippa. Despite visiting the bar most nights, she didn't see or manage to accidentally bump into her again. Finally, she asked the barman who told her that he thought she had some kind of breakdown. He kindly gave Lucy Pippa's address. She was surprised that no one had done a welfare check. The following day Lucy sent flowers with a simple get well soon message.

Pippa called Lucy the next day. She was thrilled to hear her voice. They met for coffee and quickly became friends. The shopped regularly and chatted about everything. Pippa told her that she lived with woman called Shirley. She made it very clear that they were not together, but that Shirley was a housekeeper. It was all that Lucy could do to stop herself from telling Pippa how wonderful she was and how desperately she wanted to hold her tight in her arms and kiss her sweet lips.

Over a drink one Saturday night Pippa said that she could not see Lucy anymore. That she was becoming romantically attracted to her, but that she was in a relationship. She confessed that Shirley was her lover and not a housekeeper.

Lucy told her how devastated she felt. How she allowed herself to fall deeply for her and that Pippa should have told the truth at the beginning. There were a few tears and Pippa left.

***

At 3am Sunday morning there was a knock on Lucy's front door. It was Pippa carrying a suitcase. "This is all my stuff," she told Lucy, "and I'm moving in." Lucy invited her in and made them both a coffee.

"I think you need to go away for a week, sleep alone, and think about what you really want and then if you still feel the same way call me."

Pippa smiled and left.

***

The following Saturday flowers were delivered to Lucy's home with a C-90 cassette tape. On it were handwritten the words 'Play me Loud'.

Lucy placed the beautiful red roses into a vase and smiled before placing the cassette into her tape deck. She pressed play and waited. A song started, it was Madonna's 'Crazy for You'. Lucy could feel a lump in the back of her throat. It was all that she hoped and dreamt for and more. This wonderful, fun, crazy woman had chosen to be with her.

The phone rang.

"Hello Lucy, It's Pippa. I know what I do want and what I don't. I've made some big decisions and I'd very much like you to have dinner with me tonight at Nardiello's the Italian restaurant in the High Street."

"Okay," replied Lucy sheepishly, "I'll be there about 7.30."

"Great, I'll see you tonight."

"Pippa?"

"Yes?"

"Thank you for the recording."

"Can't wait to see you Lucy, bye."

Lucy spent the afternoon getting ready. Her nails were perfectly manicured, and her hairdresser had moved some of his clients around to fit her in. It was just after 7pm and she was checking herself in the mirror again for the third time. She wore her fuchsia pink mini skirt over black leggings, a new oversized, short sleeved, black top with a green border and a low-slung black studded belt. She had treated herself to new pair of super large, crystal styled earrings that hung right down to her shoulders. Lucy smiled, she looked and felt good. There was a car toot outside, it was the taxi. Lucy had decided to leave the car at home, so she could relax and enjoy her first date with Pippa.

***

It was just after 7.30pm when Lucy got out of the taxi outside the Italian restaurant. She entered the restaurant and was greeted with a warm handshake and a smile.

"Hello, you must be Lucy. I am Raphael Nardiello, welcome to my restaurant."

"Thank you," Lucy smiled and scanned the restaurant, "I'm meeting someone."

"Yes, I know, you are a friend of Pippa. Let me show you to your table."

Lucy was shown to a beautifully laid out corner table. Raphael pulled out the chair and Lucy sat down.

"Thank you," said Lucy.

"Hi Lucy, sorry I'm a few minutes late."

It was Pippa. Lucy was smitten. She looked stunning. Pippa wore black leather jacket with bright red cuffs, a black top with a matching red belt. Her black, pleated mini skirt, was short and showed her black tight cladded legs perfectly. Her black high heels shaped her calves and bottom. Pippa was as delicious as she was perplexing. Pippa slipped off her black lace, fingerless gloves and handed her jacket to Raphael.

"Wow!" said Lucy. "You look amazing!"

"Thank you and I must say you look even better than image I've kept in my head for the last week."

Lucy blushed.

"Ladies," said Raphael approaching their table, "can I get you an aperitif or maybe something from the bar?"

"We would both like one of your Negroni Cocktails please." Pippa turned to Lucy, "You'll like these Lucy. It really is the perfect Italian cocktail. It's made up with a measure of gin, Vermouth, Rosso Campari and then garnished with orange peel."

"That sounds wonderful."

Raphael handed the girls a menu each.

"Raphael, while we're reading your menu could you please send over a few nibbles?"

"Certainly Pippa," nodded Raphael leaving them to themselves.

"Do you like Italian food Lucy?"

"It's my favourite. I was thrilled when you chose here. It's a place I've wanted to dine at for some time but have never been."

"Maybe it's because you didn't have the right person to share the experience with," said Pippa smiling softly.

The girls read through the menu, ate the nibbles and sipped the cocktail. 'It's bliss,' thought Lucy.

"Are you ready to order ladies?" asked Raphael, back at the table.

"Yes," said Pippa, 'can you put together a selection of starters to share and please include your bruschetta con crema di avocada. Lucy, Raphael's avocado and smoked salmon with paprika bruschetta is too die for."

"Sounds fabulous."

"For my main," said Pippa flicking through the menu, "I'd like your white truffles with tagliatelle."

"That's a good choice," nodded Raphael.

"I would like," said Lucy placing the menu on the table, 'pollo del cacciatore. I like chicken," she smiled.

"Would you like to see a wine a list ladies?"

"No thank you," answered Pippa. "What would you recommend?'

Raphael grinned.

"I would suggest a bottle of Barolo. It's a good heavy red wine created in the Piedmont area of Italy and is made from the Nebbiolo grape. It's rich with a strong acidity and a chocolate, mint and berry flavour. It's a wine I feel would complement both your dishes."

"Then Barolo it is, thank you Raphael."

Lucy took a sip from her Cocktail.

"You said earlier that you knew what you did and didn't want. That sounded deep. Like there had been some serious soul searching."

Pippa emptied her glass and motioned Raphael to bring her another.

"I've spent my life meandering through a series of relationships with girls who were wonderful, charming, smart and beautiful. All these girls were perfect for somebody, but not right for me. What about you Lucy?"

Lucy took a deep silent breath.

"I believe in love. The forever kind. My ideal girlfriend would be curious and thoughtful but not cynical. A girl who believes in love, even though, even when and even now. I'm not interested in short term and let's see how it goes. I'm not your casual kind of girl."

"Lucy, that was incredibly direct and honest. I don't think anyone has ever been so open, with me, like that before."

"For me Pippa, if you say something that isn't true then you get something that isn't right."

"I feel the same."

"I believe in the power of language. I truly believe that miracles can and do happen when you communicate with clarity and honesty," Lucy continued.

Pippa reached across the table and touched Lucy's hand. "You're an amazing human being Lucy and a very special girl."

Lucy fell in love there and then. There was no effort. It was simple, and she could only see it getting simpler. This was love, a true honest and deep love.

Lucy and Pippa ate their meal and both chose a tiramisu for dessert. Pippa ordered two Amarettos to help them wash it down.

"I wasn't sure if you were a friend of Dorothy at first," said Pippa with a romantic glint in her eyes.

"Friend of Dorothy? I'm not sure I know a Dorothy." Pippa laughed loudly.

"That's just something we gay girls say to each other. Rather than meeting someone and asking outright are you gay or are you a lesbian, you can just slip into the conversation are you a friend of Dorothy. You know Dorothy from The Wizard of Oz."

"Oh, I get it," said Lucy smiling back shyly.

"I have an idea. There's a club not too far from here. It's called the Kissing Fish. Why don't we take a wander along, have a drink and maybe a dance?"

"I'd like that. I've not heard of the club before."

"That's because it's underground. There're no big signs. It's a small club where friends of Dorothy meet once a fortnight and enjoy each other's company without judgement or staring from straight onlookers. It's a special place for romantic drinks, people watching, relaxing and having fun."

"Okay, let's go then," said Lucy thinking how lovely Pippa looked with her big shoulder pads, olive coloured skin and long dark hair. She was elegant and yet her every movement just oozed sex appeal.

"Can we have the bill please Raphael?" called Pippa. Lucy reached down for her handbag.

"Absolutely not. This evening is on me," she said standing up unsteadily. "Whoops," she laughed resting against the chair, "that may be one Amaretto too many too soon."

The taxi stopped outside a hotel and Lucy followed Pippa around to a set of stairs that led down to the club. Lucy was excited, she could feel her adrenalin racing around her body. She thought how impossible it was that a place like this existed and right in the middle of her town. It was real, she had never been to a gay club before. She smiled broadly and told herself I'm going to a gay club and, I'm going with Pippa.

Pippa paid the entrance fee and Lucy followed her inside. The sound of Wham blasted out I'm Your Man in the quirky club which was decorated in a mix of golds and red. It was vibrant and trendy. There were girls everywhere, as couples, in groups and dancing together on the dance floor. Lucy had not prepared herself. The mix of emotions she felt, the heavy beating in her chest and the sweatiness of her palms. She could not believe she was surrounded by so many girls who liked girls.

Pippa took her by the hand and led her through to the champagne bar. She motioned the barman over.

"We'll take a couple of your very own Cosmos please Billy."
"Cosmos?" quizzed Lucy.

"Oh you will love these Lucy. Right now, the Cosmopolitan is the gayest drink the world! It's made with vodka, triple sec, cranberry juice and freshly squeezed lime juice."

Billy placed the drinks on the bar.

"Now this will make you laugh because there are bar tenders in San Francisco, New York and Miami that claim to have invented the Cosmo. But, we have it on good authority that Billy here from Exeter City was in fact the true inventor."

The girls laughed and took a sip from their drinks.

"Pippa, I've never been anywhere quite like this. It's amazing! So many people, just like us, in one place."

"Well like us isn't quite right. You see there are no stereotypical friends of Dorothy. It takes all sorts. For example, can you see that woman over there," she pointed to a woman standing alone at the bar, "that is what we call a desperation number. Just before closing time she's the one racing around trying to find a sex partner. Her interest is casual sex, nothing else. Then there's the Gillette Blade," she pointed to a blond, short haired woman dancing in a group. She's a bisexual. She likes guys and girls. Once a fortnight she'll leave her mundane heterosexual life at home, become the person she'd like to be every day of the week and make her way here to get her needy fix of girl on girl action."

"What about that one?" Lucy pointed to an older woman in the company of two younger girls.

"Oh, that's Valerie, she's an eyeball queen." "An eyeball queen, what's that then?"

"Valerie derives her pleasure from watching others engage in sexual intercourse. Watching is more important than playing for her. I've heard she holds some pretty wild parties."

"What about her?" Lucy nodded towards a dark, short haired girl with long slender legs.

"We would call her an Iron Closet. She's probably married with children and lies to herself every day that the life she has is the one she wants. Sadly, she's in denial and may never come out and live her life as a truly happy gay woman."

"So, what would others call me?" said Lucy raising an eyebrow.

"That's easy, there's no real name for you but I'd call you an ice cream."

"An ice cream?"

"Sure, because you're so sweet a person could easily get this overwhelming desire to just lick you."

The record changed. It was I Will Survive by Gloria Gaynor.

"Come on," said Pippa grabbing Lucy by the hand. "Let's dance."

Lucy followed Pippa out to the dance floor. It was as if every girl in the club was there, all thrusting their arms up into the air and singing loudly along. The feeling of solidarity was unlike anything Lucy had ever experienced before. Today was a day when Lucy awoke, yesterdays were gone, and tomorrows would never be the same again. As the song finished the DJ played Madonna's Into the Groove. Everyone swayed as one on the dance floor. Lucy closed her eyes and just let the music and atmosphere envelope her.

"Hey Pippa," called a great looking redheaded girl dressed in a sexy black glittery mini dress, "your girlfriend is awesome!"

"I know," Pippa called back with a grin.

Lucy couldn't help but think there was such sincerity in the redhead's voice.

The record ended, and the girls returned to the champagne bar.

"Can we have two more Cosmos please Billy?" asked Lucy with excitement in her voice.

Billy nodded.

"Oh, so you're becoming a Cosmo expert now," joked Pippa.

"I sure am," she said brightly. "I'm rapidly becoming a Cosmo drinking ice cream who also happens to be a good friend of Dorothy."

"You're bloody amazing," said Pippa smiling. She leant forward and gently kissed Lucy on the cheek.

As Trapped by Colonel Abrams finished the DJ slowed the pace down and played Move Closer by Phyliss Nelson.

Pippa took Lucy's hand. "Will you dance with me?"

Lucy beamed and followed her back onto the dance floor. She placed her arms around Pippa's neck. Pippa did the same around Lucy's waist. They both slowly swayed to the music of their first slow dance. Lucy placed her head gently against Pippa's chest. She smiled to herself thinking how she was now dancing with the girl of her dreams.

Pippa whispered into her ear. "Just twelve hours ago everything in my life was just so normal, so boring. Now, with you, everything feels vibrant, unexpected, delightful and literally forever changed."

"I never saw this coming Pippa."

"Me neither Lucy. It's like nothing else in the world matters. Not the job, family, nothing. I just want to immerse myself in a world filled with our love."

"This feels reckless, careless and my emotional barriers are nowhere to be found but I don't care. I think I've fallen in love with you Pippa."

"I've been waiting for a girl like you all my life Lucy. I love you."

Lucy looked up at Pippa lips, she dropped her gaze and her eyelids and then slowly looked back at Pippa with a welcoming smile. Pippa swept Lucy's hair from her face and drew her gently towards her soft and slightly parted lips.

The kiss ended with an intimate short silence. Lucy hugged Pippa and whispered, "Shall we go home?"

Chapter 29

Lucy, Pauline and few of their friends had decided to meet with a psychic. After much chat and prevarication, they concluded it would be fun and an opportunity to get together for a few glasses of wine and a natter. One of the girls, Fay, had met with Allison Coffey the psychic and had raved about her predictions for months. Lucy was a little sceptical but decided to be open minded and enjoy the experience.

"Good evening ladies. My name is Allison Coffey. For those who know little or nothing about the mystic way I communicate telepathically with my angels and spirit guides who read and interpret your aura. That's the spiritual light surrounding your physical body. I can also communicate with your angels and spirit guides. Most people have several of each. Through me, these angels and spirit guides convey the information that is most needed and desired by you. I want to put your minds at rest now. All my readings are positive and constructive in nature. I will answer your personal questions pertaining to love, physical and mental health issues, relationships, soul mates, business, career. I will cover most things that important to you which may include your life's purpose, your undiscovered talents as well as past incarnations and how they relate to this life. I can, if it's what you want, help you to identify and communicate with, and feel the presence of your guardian angels, spirit guides as well as deceased loved ones."

Lucy took a long sip from her glass and watched the other ladies chatting.

"Hello." Allison held out her hand to Lucy and shook it. "I'm drawn to you. I feel we should talk first. Is that okay?"

Lucy smiled awkwardly and answered, "Sure I'm Lucy."

Lucy followed Allison through the lounge, up the stairs and into the bedroom. Lucy sensed a very calming atmosphere in the room. It felt like a place of safety. Allison sat on the corner of the bed and revealed a pen and paper.

"I like to make some notes while I'm communicating. Sometimes the messages come through fast and I don't want you to miss something important. Are you ready?"

"Yes, I'm ready."

"Okay. Oh my, you have seven spirit guides. They tell me you've recently met someone. A person that is special, like no other. You want to know if things are serious between you. I can tell you that you will love this person forever. I can't say that you will be together forever, that's not clear, but that person, that woman, will stay in your heart until you leave this place and move on to the spirit world. You are very lucky to have met this woman. I feel that you met each other in a previous life. I sense strongly you are long lost soul mates who have found each other again. The love you have found is very difficult to find but so easy to lose. Does that make sense?" asked Allison scribbling furiously on her note pad.

"Yes, it does. Thank you."

"You are where you are supposed to be in your career. I don't think you consciously chose the path. I'm sensing police force or military. It was not what you initially wanted but that is the right path for you. You are bright, intelligent. Oh my, very intelligent. I'm told that you have something special. The ability to see things and recall them easily."

"Yes, I have photographic memory. It's not something I usually talk about. But yes, I read something and then see that picture in my head."

"Please, don't tell me too much Lucy. You have been involved in lots of very difficult situations in your job, lots of heartache, violence and misery. But I'm told you have been a good Samaritan and helped and saved many poor spirits on their life's journey. You will go far in your career, you will strengthen relationships with co-workers although I sense strongly that you do not suffer fools gladly. There will be conflict, but you will remain steadfast and see whatever challenge is presented through. You will always have money, you work hard and save for the future. I sense you're thinking about buying a home, maybe with someone. Buying the home is the right thing to do.

It will, for now, make you happy. I don't see you always in this country, maybe Spain but definitely somewhere with a warm climate. I sense, strongly, that things have not always been right with your mum but you've both been working hard at getting the relationship to where it should be. I'm told that this is a good thing for you both. I sense strongly an overwhelming feeling of love and understanding. Your spirit guides tell me that your mum loves you Lucy. She may not have always been able to show it but her love now is unconditional. I'm getting a message, wait a minute, yes, yes okay. Your spirit guide wants you to take a deep soothing breath. You do not have to shoulder the whole load. There is nothing that you do or are involved in that requires you to be the only one in charge. Not everything has to start and end with you. You are very capable and beautiful in manner and countenance, and at the same time you are not alone. We are always available and with you, by your side. You do not need to try and prove to us or any group of human beings what you can do for we know this to be true. Your life's mission is so valid, so delicious. Allow this mission to feed and nourish you. Let it take you to the full extent of what and who you are in the big scheme of things. Attempt not to strangle your life force and focus, by working so hard at simply being. Being is your natural state and flows so smoothly when you are relaxed and at ease with letting it all happen through the grace of all that is. We know that you know this. I am one of your spirit guides, I wish not to scold or chastise you but simply offering and reminding you about a flower to be opened and adored. You are a delightful human individual and woman. Remember your joy at being in peace. It is what you always exude. Sometimes by choosing effort rather than being, you short cut your purpose and your physical being. Does that make sense Lucy?"

"Yes, I think so."

"I'm not sure if I should tell you this." "Tell me what?"

"I'm getting a message. I can see a rose, you're being handed a rose. It wasn't bought from a shop; the hand that gave it would never have had the money to shop but he gave you thought. He wanted to give something. Something that said thank you for your kindness. I can feel cold, freezing cold. The person has passed. He passed recently, very recently. He didn't mean to do it, he didn't want to die but he wants to thank you. He wants very much to thank you."

"Allison, I don't know anyone that has died recently."

"This is very recent. He's not family but someone you've been kind to. It will all make sense in the fullness of time. Is there anything specific you want to ask me?"

"No, I think you've given me plenty to think about. Thank you."

Allison handed Lucy her notes and asked her to send the next person up.

Lucy took a long sip from her wine and told Pauline she had to leave as she was on duty shortly. She had brought her uniform, so she could go straight to the nick.

***

Outside the station Lucy heard her name being called. "Hi, you must be Lucy Penfold."

"I am, can I help you?"

"I'm not sure you can. I'm Shirley and you may or probably haven't heard of me?"

Shirley was a large woman, well built with short black hair. She had a nice smile and looked almost boyish.

"Shirley, no I can't say I have."

"I didn't think so. Not that it matters. Until very recently I was with Pippa."

"Okay, yes Pippa did mention you."

"Don't worry I haven't come to cause a scene. Unless you want to arm wrestle for her," she laughed out loud. "Hey, Pippa and I had fun, but it ran its course. I never expected to tame her and go the distance. There are things that we both need to sort out regarding the flat. I've had to give notice as I can't afford the rent on my own and she's entitled to half the deposit."

"Have you found somewhere else?"

"No, that's a real problem. There just isn't anything ready right now to move in to. I mean look at it we're right on top of Christmas, its freezing cold and the last thing any sensible person would want to do is move right now."

"Listen, you seem like a nice person Shirley. If I speak with Pippa and she's okay with it do you think you could bear to share with us.? I mean until the New Year and you get yourself sorted with your own flat."

"What, really? You'd do that for me?"

"Yeah of course. It's not like we're kids in the playground fighting over someone's affection. It's unorthodox but, providing Pippa's okay, you can stay with us."

"I'm really touched, thank you. I can see how Pippa could fall for you, you have a big heart. I didn't expect this. I promise to be the best house guest a person could be."

"Okay, I'm on duty now. I'll call you later once I've had a chance to speak with Pippa."

***

Lucy had only been in the Panda car when she received a radio call to attend a disturbance at the Girls Reform Home. A place referred to, by the many girls Lucy had encountered, as Colditz. Lucy was the first one on the scene. There were over thirty teenage girls in the grounds. A staff member ran towards the car.

"Thank God, you're here officer. These girls are out of control. They've defied staff, smashed windows and doors and have refused to obey orders. One girl, yes that one there," she pointed, "Hannah Graves, threatened to attack a staff member with a knife and then grabbed another and held her by the throat. She was choking, she couldn't breath and when one of my staff tried to help she wrestled her down and bit her on the arm, her teeth penetrated the flesh and bone. She's in a bad way."

"Okay, what started all this?" asked Pippa calmly.

"Nothing out of the unusual. It doesn't take much to light the fuse in a place like this."

Lucy turned and walked towards the group of girls. A short, overweight girl with short cropped hair charged towards her screaming with a rock in her hand. Lucy stood her ground, grabbed the girls arm and used her own motion to throw her over her hip into a heap on the ground. Lucy leant her knee on the back of the girl's head, pulled her arms tight behind her back and handcuffed her prisoner. Lucy got up and stepped forward again.

"That didn't need to happen," she said casually with open arms. "I was hoping to talk with you girls."

"Is that you Lucy?"

"That's right, it's me WPC Lucy Penfold."

"She's alright, she is. I mean for a copper. You can trust her Gabby," said one of the girls.

"So, are you in charge then Gabby?"

A tall, slim, pretty, dark blond girl wearing blue jean dungarees and trainers stepped forward. "I'm Gabby and no I'm not in charge. That's the job of the staff."

"What is the problem Gabby? How did we find ourselves in this situation?"

"Like you're interested."

"I'm here Gabby and I'm listening. I know that something like this doesn't just happen because there's another repeat on the television."

"Not everyone here is a mindless criminal. Now Hannah the Spanner, that's the girl you've just handcuffed. She's way past saving. Her life is mapped out before her and it'll be one disaster after another with nothing but bloodshed, heartache and tears. Most of us, and I do mean most of us, committed crimes to escape violent fathers, fearless mothers, violent beatings and being molested. We end up here because neighbours, teachers and friends didn't listen, and we couldn't face the pain anymore. We had to escape."

"I understand that you're not all criminals, but you have been sent, by the authorities, to this place and this," Lucy pointed to the broken windows, "isn't acceptable."

"Do you really understand WPC Lucy Penfold? Do you understand that we're carrying around severe emotional wounds and frightening experiences? We're trying to cope with traumas that have disrupted the path of our physical, spiritual and intellectual development. Girls in here have suffered from emotional, physical and sexual abuse, neglect, family violence, racism and abandonment. Could you really understand how overwhelmed some of us are and that it can be beyond our capacity to cope? We're harbouring powerful feelings of fear, terror, lack of control and for some complete despair. What you have here, WPC Lucy Penfold, are victims who try desperately to use distraction like poor behaviour or truancy for self-healing, to try and get to a positive place. This here, is a consequence to something that happened to each and every one of us. We didn't choose this life."

"Okay Gabby, I'm clearly dealing with an articulate, intelligent individual with the vocabulary to express herself. How can we fix this? I don't want this to get nasty and I don't believe you do either."

"We all accept that we have been sent here. We accept that the authorities don't care about our individual situations. We've been lumped together as criminals but the way we're being treated here is what really isn't acceptable. The discipline and punishment doesn't fit the crime. The law states that no young offender should be placed in confinement for no more than three days. I personally have been locked away for twenty-one days. Yes, that's right twenty-one days solid in a room with no light or windows and fed just milk and two slices of bread. My crime? No more than writing and encouraging others to blow the whistle on the humiliation and violence we are subjected to here, to our parents, friends, the newspapers, in fact anyone who will listen. This isn't just about me. Every one of us girls have suffered the whippings. Again, the law states that a young offender should have no more than three lashes across the palm of your open hand. Now either the staff here can't count and don't know an arse from a hand but twenty lashes across the backside isn't unusual. I've seen weaker girls here on the brink of suicide. We had to take action!"

"Has anybody responded to your letters Gabby?"

"No and do you know why? They were read by the staff here and burnt. A few of us were made an example of with bare arse lashings in front of everyone. Finally, we were ordered to write letters that said we were happy and being well looked after. The quality and quantity of our daily meals were reduced. We were being openly and systematically chastised. Can you imagine how we felt? It left me in a place where I didn't even cry anymore and that scares me. This is our last hope to draw attention to a criminal act being carried out on societies victims that are labelled young offenders."

"I've listened to everything you've said Gabby and I promise to make it my business to ensure there is a full and comprehensive investigation carried out here. Can I ask you please to cease what you're doing and help us all to get this situation cleared up?"

"We're trusting you Lucy Penfold to do the right thing."

The altercation came to an end. Lucy knew what she had to do. She would not give her word and then fail to deliver.

***

Back at the nick Lucy phoned Pippa who agreed to Shirley staying until she organised another apartment in the New Year. In the bar she overheard two CID officers laughing about an old tramp who had bled to death. She discovered it was Roger Harris, a homeless person she met on a night shift and had befriended while out on foot patrol. He was an ex-soldier: a happy, nice old man. Lucy would often make two rounds of sandwiches and crisps then sit and eat with him. He would tell her stories about his life and Lucy would listen. One evening he gave Lucy a red rose that he'd picked from a garden. He thanked her for giving him her time and listening. It was winter and bitterly cold. Roger would often commit a crime during this time of the year to escape the bitter weather eat good hot food. This year he had taken a sharp object and slit his wrists then called 999 from a phone box. He bled to death before anyone reached him. Lucy stormed back into the bar and looked at the officers laughing and enjoying their drink in the comfort of a centrally heated room.

"You pair are heartless bastards. I don't know how you live with yourselves!"

Chapter 30

<---------->

"Thank you for tonight. I just love the food at Nardiello's and the special service we get is fabulous," said Lucy as she pulled the bed covers up.

"Hey, you're welcome, now get your cute bottom over here for a hug."

Lucy snuggled in tight. "I love you like crazy Pippa. I honestly believe that we have a true meeting of minds."

"The only meeting of minds I want is the banging of the headboard," laughed Pippa.

"You are so naughty," she whispered. "Do you know the strangest thing happened at work the other day"

"What was that?"

"Well there was this girl in the canteen and she was just watching me. Not in a bad way. I ignored it for a while but every time I looked around she was just, well you know looking. I went over and said hello and she was full of smiles and asked me to join her. We chatted for a while and then she invited me to dinner. I thanked her and asked if I could bring my partner along. She looked at me like I'd taken the last Jaffa Cake from the plate. Without saying another word, she just got up and walked off."

"She must have fancied you."

"Really?"

"Yes, really and I bet you enjoyed the attention, didn't you?"

"No and it didn't dawn on me that she could be gay."

"What, so come to bed eyes from across the canteen didn't ring alarm bells?"

"No Pippa, like I said I found the whole thing quite bizarre."

"So, what happened next, did you follow her out and take her number?"

"Where did that come from Pippa? I would never do anything like that."

"So, have you seen her since or are you building up to a confession that you've been sleeping with the bitch."

"Pippa, what the hell are you talking about? I just told you about something strange. I shared that with you openly and honestly. I have no interest in anyone but you. Surely you must know Pippa, you are the love of my life, the centre of my universe."

"Okay, I love you too Lucy."

"Good, now let's not spoil another great night over something so trivial and meaningless. Okay?"

"Alright, I'm feeling tired now and want to go to sleep."

"Are you sure Pippa, are you sure you don't want to, well you know?" asked Lucy in a soft whisper.

"Not now Lucy, I'm really tired and need to be up in the morning. Good night."

Lucy turned the light off. She tried to sleep but found herself going over the conversation in her head. She couldn't comprehend how an innocent remark had so quickly spoilt the mood. An hour later and Lucy was still awake. Then just as she felt herself slipping away into sleep she thought she heard a sound downstairs. She stayed completely still in the dark listening intently for any noise. She heard something.

Lucy got out of bed and slipped on her dressing gown. She shook Pippa and placed her hand gently over her mouth as she woke and signalled with her finger to stay quiet. Opening the bedroom door Lucy crept to the top of the stairs. She could hear noises in the lounge now quite clearly. Lucy slowly and quietly walked down the stairs. The sound of drawers opening and muffled talk was now much clearer. Lucy opened the door and turned on the light. In front of her were two white males in their early twenties. The taller of the two carried a crow bar. They turned, startled to see Lucy standing at the door. One dropped his bag and ran towards Lucy. Using her martial arts training she side stepped him, grabbed his arm and kicked the back of his knees. He was on the ground with his arm pulled up tight behind his back. The burglar yelped in pain. Pippa had followed her down the stairs. She saw what was happening and scrambled to find her handcuffs. She threw them over and her prisoner was cuffed in seconds.

"You'd best put that crow bar down!" commanded Lucy! The burglar held it tighter and lifted it to shoulder height.

"You're in big trouble now. You've only gone and burgled a police officer's house."

"You better let us fucking go bitch or I'll do yer!"

"That's not going to happen sunshine. Burglars like you are scum, the lowest of the low. You steal from good, honest, hard- working people because you're too damn lazy to get a job and contribute like the rest of us. I've met hundreds of the victims you leave behind. They're upset, afraid, unsettled and confused. I have known families, happy families who have become so traumatised after a burglary that they have moved home."

"I'm warning you!"' growled the burglar raising the crow bar above his head.

"Last week," Lucy continued calmly, "I visited an old lady who was clearly powerless and vulnerable. Burglars had beaten her for just £40. She was hospitalised with serious injuries to her arms, chest and face. That poor innocent woman died three days later. So, no you can shake that crowbar and make all the threats you like but you're not leaving here."

The burglar became increasingly agitated. He looked down at the floor and saw his partner cuffed and then at Lucy who was now holding the house phone and calling the incident in.

"I had nothing to do with the old lady. I don't think I've ever robbed an old lady's house in my life."

"Good, I'm pleased to hear that."

"So, let us go then please, and we'll never see each other again."

Lucy shook her head.

"The best that I can do is to have you charged with burglary but, if you don't drop that crowbar now and I do mean now, then under section 10 of the 1986 theft act what you have there is an offensive weapon which will guarantee you'll do time."

"I don't want to go to prison, please I don't want either of us to go to prison."

"Then drop it now!"

The burglar dropped the crowbar. Pippa handed her a pair of handcuffs.

"Pippa," she whispered, "you'd better make yourself scarce. If those above us think that we're living together then we'll both be in trouble. Call me in a couple of hours when this is all wrapped up."

Pippa nodded and left the room.

Lucy walked cautiously towards the burglar, his hands were visibly shaking. "Turn around and place your hands behind you back"

He did as he was told and whimpered as Lucy cuffed him.

"You are under arrest for burglary. You do not have to say anything, but it may harm your defence if you do not mention, when questioned, something which you later rely on in court. Do you understand?"

"Yes."

A few minutes later there was a knock on the door. Lucy opened it and let Bob and two uniformed officers into her home.'

"Bloody hell Lucy, what has happened here?"

"A couple of burglars Bob." She shook her head. "They picked the wrong house to rob tonight."

Bob grabbed the larger of the burglars by the arms.

"You matey, don't know how lucky you are to still be standing here in one piece. I've known this officer to violently tear a criminal's bollocks clean off with her teeth."

The burglar winced as he was led out by the uniformed officers.

"Bob don't go saying stuff like that."

"Lucy, I'm just having a laugh. So, do you feel safe enough after all that to commotion to sleep here on your own tonight?"

"I've told you before. You've got two hopes. Bob Hope and no hope!"

"Hey, you can't blame me for trying. One of these days you may just succumb to my charms, fall head over heels in love, pack all this in and have babies with me."

"Err, nah, not in this lifetime."

"Cheers for that. Are coming down the station to write up a statement?"

"Yeah sure Bob, give me ten minutes and I'll drive down."

Chapter 31

24 months later

"Hi Pauline, thanks for meeting me."

"That's not a problem Lucy. I've been thinking about you so it's nice to catch up."

Lucy had met with Pauline for a drink at the Blackwell Arms. "Is it your mum?"

"No, no," said Lucy with a broad smile. "In fact, our relationship has blossomed. I think that we're both in a really good place now."

"That's great to hear. I'm really pleased for both of you." "I took Pippa back home to meet her."

"Wow that was brave. Did you tell her about, well you know?"

"No, definitely not but I'm pretty sure she knew. Pippa and Mother got on really well: they chatted, laughed and when it came to bed time Mother suggested that we share my old room."

"That is so good Lucy. Wow, that really is a major step forward. I couldn't be more pleased for you. So, what's on your mind?"

"It's Pippa," said Lucy, her voice quavering.

"In what way? Have you guys had an argument or a fall out?"

"It's a bit more than that. Some time ago she told me how unhappy she was that I earnt more money than her. I told her at the time that between us we had more than enough money to do whatever we wanted, and that time together was far more important."

"How did she take that?"

"It was like I was talking to myself. It seemed to bother her and every so often I'd get a snide remark about paying for something. It was like a scratch that she couldn't itch. Just as I thought things had got better she told me that there was a position with the Regional Crime Squad and it paid a lot more money but would involve her being away. Once again I told her that time for each other was far more important and we didn't need the money."

"What did she say?"

"Pauline, I couldn't believe it. She applied and got the position without saying a word. The first I heard was when she was offered and accepted the role."

"Oh dear, that's not good."

"No, it wasn't. One minute we were together and the next she's away and I get little more than a phone call saying that's she's away on a case, that she can't speak about it only that she's had to take her passport."

"It happened that quick?"

"You know me Pauline. If it had been her ambition or part of a plan to move forward then I'd completely understand and would support her. However, that wasn't it. The whole move was about my earning more money than her."

"So where are you now?"

"Pippa flits back and forth. We talk, and she brings me expensive presents back from Spain, but something just isn't right."

"How do you mean something isn't right?"

"My gut instinct tells me she's playing away?"

"What, you mean seeing other girls?"

"I really think so. I mean it wouldn't be the first time she's lied about stuff like that. When we first met she said that the girl she was living with was a housekeeper and she wasn't. I know she flirts and I mean flirts with guys and well as girls."

"I'm so sorry Lucy. Do you think she swings both ways then?"

"No. I'm pretty sure she doesn't, but during one holiday away she was flirting like mad with this Spanish guy who owned a boat. She was going right over the top with fluttering eye lashes, big smiles and cheeky laughs. I know Pippa, I know all those moves, and she did them right under my nose. Pauline, it was like I wasn't even there."

"So, did she go off on the boat with him?"

"I think she would have if I hadn't told him to sod off as Pippa was with me."

Pauline laughed. "I bet that shook him."

"Yeah," sighed Lucy, "the guy just stood there looking awkward, apologised and disappeared."

"It sounds like this has been festering a while."

"It has Pauline. I'm just not completely sure if she's being unfaithful to me."

"To be honest and frank with you Lucy I'm not sure what causes one person to cheat on the person they claim to love. It could be that they're self-absorbed, selfish or maybe there's something dysfunctional lurking beneath their deceptive ways. I do believe that most cheaters are narcissists or at the very least share many similar qualities."

"In what way?" quizzed Lucy.

"Well they are selfish, greedy and often only think only of themselves. Typically, the person feels a sense of entitlement and will do whatever necessary to feed their desires. So, the question is, can Pippa be a little self-absorbed or maybe she's just looking out for number one and lacks empathy? Do you think Pippa could have affairs without feeling guilty?"

Lucy sat upright.

"I do think Pippa can behave like that and if history is anything to go by then could she have an affair without any thought for me. I think, probably, yes."

"Is Pippa the kind of girl that could look you straight in the eyes and tell a lie without even blinking?"

"Yes, I believe she could. In the past she has told stories that are so outrageous that you just can't help but believe them."

"The thing is Lucy, we tend to believe these people because they have perfected the lie, which can sound utterly convincing. I've seen it in domestic cases, you must have too. Their lives are so full of deception that the line between truth and fiction is blurred. I'm not saying that all liars are cheaters, but you can't be a cheater and not be a liar, the two go hand in hand."

"You're right. I've seen that dozens of times at domestic call outs. The truth looks so obvious to us looking in, but the wife just goes along with the lies."

"Cheaters will constantly question you and frequently accuse you of inappropriate behaviour or being flirtatious. The very fact that are capable of being unfaithful puts them on the defensive and paranoia sets in. It's almost like they think that if they're doing it their partner must be doing it too. They are so deep into their lives of lies and deception that insecurity sets in that they'll begin accusing partners of all sorts of things. I've said to wives in the past, when I've worked domestics, to always listen carefully to what your husband is saying. The chances are they are projecting what they are doing. On one occasion I told this woman that if her husband says that you were late last night and were probably having it off with someone in the office then what they really mean is I am late sometimes because I'm banging the secretary. My advice was to tune themselves into their cheating behaviour by listening hard and sooner or later you'll start figuring out what they're up to by what they accuse you of."

"Pippa and I have had words in the past. I never really thought about it."

"From what I've seen Lucy, a common trait among cheaters is their constant need for more. That can be money, attention, recognition. They are never happy or satisfied. They need constant attention and frequent ego boosts. Lucy, I have attended domestic situations where a husband has been violent towards a wife because their new born child is receiving more attention than him. These kinds of people are never happy, no matter what they have in their lives. No matter how much you give they will always need more. They have to be the centre of attention. They have to feel needed and wanted always."

"There's a lot of Pippa in there. There have been times when we've been with friends at a dinner party and someone has just told a desperately sad story, like their father has just been diagnosed with cancer and Pippa would start telling them about the new sports car she was going to buy. It did take me back at the time, but it passed. Like so many things I suppose."

Pauline shook her head.

"Cheaters, Lucy, are most often, but not always huge flirts. They need validation from and to be desired by others and by the sounds of it, Pippa needs that from both sexes. They can see the simple exchange as an invitation for more. I'm not so sure that it's because they have huge egos but that they lack self-esteem. It's not unusual for them to flirt in front of you, just as you said about the Spanish guy, as they see it as harmless fun. It's almost like they think if a person sees it with their own eyes then it'd never happen behind their backs. In my opinion Lucy flirting is disrespectful under any circumstances and is a huge red flag."

"I don't know what to say Pauline, so much of what you're saying has or is happening."

"I can only tell you what I've seen and experienced from the job, but it does seem that the saddest part of a cheater's personality is that they often carry emotional scars from their past. So many unfaithful partners turn out to be emotionally abused as children, were ignored or had love attention withheld. Sometimes it can be that their own parents were just messed up relationships. It's almost like the very thing they crave most, attention, is the thing that causes them to cheat in the first place. Their fear of being alone is so huge that they need a backup plan. They need to know that someone is available to them. I've seen woman who believed that their husband's emotional dependence was so high that he wouldn't risk losing them by having an affair. The catch here is that their insecurity is so strong they need to have affairs, so they never feel alone or insignificant. Lucy, I know that you said Pippa has confessed to having cheated in the past. To me that indicates the extent of her moral code. She has pretty much told you that she's prepared to cross the line and will likely do it again. I'm not saying that Pippa is cheating on you Lucy only sharing what I've learnt along life's merry way. Even if what you both had is over, then unhappy or not, partners deserve a better ending to their relationship than infidelity. This is clearly on your mind Lucy and it's something that will need to address. You are a good person Lucy Penfold, do not make excuses to yourself for poor behaviour. It's not acceptable, do not tolerate it. If you do not stand for something, then you will fall for anything. Be strong, you do not have to live that way."

Lucy rested her head into her hands. "She slapped me Pauline. We had an argument about something silly, and it was my birthday, and she just slapped me hard around the face. As I looked at her in shock. For a few seconds I couldn't see Pippa. Not the Pippa who I fell in love with and that wasn't the only time. She also scratched my face and made me bleed. It took almost four months to heal. There have been other occasions when she has just gone mad and started throwing cups and plates at me. It was like she became someone else. That look in her eyes was scary, not my Pippa."

Pauline became agitated. "That is bloody unacceptable. She had no right, no right whatsoever!"

***

Later that night Pippa returned from an overseas assignment. "Hey Lucy, are you home?"

"Yeah, I'm home Pippa. I wasn't expecting you," said Lucy walking out from the kitchen.

"I've got you a present, come and take a look at these beauties," said Pippa revealing a small box wrapped with a small red bow. Pippa showed her the box and then opened it.

"These are real pearls Lucy. You'll look great wearing these."

"Pippa, I still don't understand why you're doing this."

"Doing what?"

"Why you joined the Regional Crime Squad.'

"I've told you. It wasn't right that I was a detective and you earned a lot more money than me. It made me feel lower than you, so I changed it"

"But I told you, it's our money for our life together. Now I don't see you from one week to the next. You're separating us Pippa, is money more important than me?"

"Well just look what the extra money can bring in. Now you have a pair of real pearl earrings plus I bought you back two bottles of Poison perfume from duty free."

"You're missing the point Pippa."

"What bloody point Lucy? What more do you want?"

"I think you've been seeing someone else."

Pippa paused for a few seconds and let out a wry smile.

"If you can't commit to us as a couple who claim to love each other then you best just go Pippa. Have an affair and enjoy yourself."

"Okay, yes I have been seeing other girls, several in fact. They didn't mean anything. It was just the thrill of the chase and sex. No romance, no love or tender kisses, just pure sex."

"Well that's it then Pippa, you need to leave now. Whatever we had is gone. We're done!"

"Look I know and understand you're upset right now but let's stay friends, don't be a stranger Lucy." Pippa turned, collected her case and left.

Lucy fell back into her armchair. All that she believed they had was over. This wasn't the Pippa she'd been sharing a life with. She reached for the phone.

"Hello."

"Hello Pauline, it's Lucy. I've spoken with Pippa, she confessed all and has left."

"Stay where you are, I'm on my way."

Lucy hung up the phone. In what seemed like a few minutes there was knock at the door. In what seemed like a dream state Lucy rose and opened it.

"Come here Lucy.'" said Pauline throwing her arms around her. Come on take a seat and I'll pour us both a glass of wine."

The girls sat together. Lucy explained what had happened and took a long sip from the wine glass.

"Lucy, moving on from something like this can seem like an impossible task. I think the first thing you need to do is allow yourself to feel everything; that's bitterness, sorrow, confusion and in moderation maybe a touch of rage. It may all seem quite raw as we sit here now but you will find the need to move on and not let what's happened define you. The facts of life are that we don't get to control the crappy things that people can do but we can control how we respond."

"I just can't believe she would do that to me Pauline, I was and probably still am deeply and madly in love with her. I found myself thinking, just before you arrived, maybe if I had been stronger, smarter, shorter, more beautiful, less successful then she wouldn't have sought out another woman."

"Lucy, that's bullshit. Since when is anybody responsible for somebody else's happiness? If we make someone happy then great, but it should never be a person's responsibility. If it wasn't now, then it would be at some point in the future. You said yourself that she had done it before, so it was always going to happen again. If you focus on the job at hand. It sounds like you made the decision to end it and she's accepted your decision. There's nothing now to argue about, who did what, where and when. If she can do that to a good, honest decent girl like you then she'll cheat on just about anyone. You, my friend Lucy Penfold, deserve to be someone who deserves and respects you."

"Thank you, Pauline. I just feel like shit right now. It's like my love has been taken, abused and violated."

Pauline poured Lucy a second glass of wine and squeezed her hand. "Affairs are built on lies and secrecy. I can only imagine that the constant guilt and torment must be unbearable. Tomorrow when Pippa wakes up from the childishness of all that she's done, it'll probably feel humiliating in the light of day. I just can't imagine her feeling good about herself."

Pauline paused for second and smiled.

"You are going to get people who tell you to forgive her and maybe that's what you'll need to do as part of the healing process. Just don't let anyone dictate the timeframe. It may sound like a mountain right now, but you will need to get on with rebuilding your new life. You will experience a rollercoaster of emotions over the coming months and you'll need to reach out to a friend who will always dispense balanced, non- judgemental advice. That will be me Lucy. I'll be here for you."

"Thank you, Pauline you really are a good friend to me. I appreciate and value all your good advice."

"Right, now on the up-side. Let's put some dates in the diary. I don't know, maybe a few nights out with the girls, join a dance class or maybe use the Gym at the station a bit more. There's no time to sit around reflecting on what may have been just what will be."

Chapter 32

"Good morning everyone. My name is Sergeant Stanley Anderson and I'm with FIU, that's Football Intelligence Unit for those who are not familiar with our work. I'm here because intelligence tells us that tomorrow's football game between Exeter City and Cardiff is likely to turn violent."

"So, with the greatest of respect," said Danny, "are you here to tell us to keep an eye on anyone wearing blue jeans, braces, Doctor Martin Boots and sporting a skinhead haircut Sergeant?"

"No, I'm here because things have moved on a long way from what you've just described as your 1970's bovver boy. The person and era you've just described are long gone. No longer are our targets obvious mindless thugs just looking for a fight with someone wearing a different scarf. Today's football hooligans have jobs, many of them very good, well paid jobs. They are managing companies or running their own businesses. Today's football hooligan wears smart designer sporting clothes. The kind of person that you," he pointed at Danny, "are most likely to rush straight passed when it kicks off."

"Do we know how large this gang is?" asked Lucy.

"They're not a gang, they call themselves a firm. Every football team around the UK has a at least one, if not more firms."

"Why a firm Sergeant?"

"It's because they run themselves like a business. Everything is extremely well organised, and members of these football firms are motivated, determined and extremely violent. We, as a force, are still catching up. We do have officers undercover with some of the major firms which is how we gather intelligence. Until the events of Luton in 1985 unfolded, football hooliganism wasn't really on the radar. However, post Luton the Prime Minister and the FA discussed a six-point plan and declared war on the hooligans."

"I'm sorry sir, what happened at Luton?"

"Carnage, utter carnage that's what happened. The FIU was still in its infancy and struggling for resources to do the job properly. It was the sixth round of the FA cup and Millwall were to play away with Luton Town. It was mid-week game and intelligence suggested that no more than five thousand fans would travelling to the ground. We got it wrong, very wrong. The FIU had already identified Millwall's Bushwackers as one of the most notorious firms in the country. An estimated ten thousand turned up in Luton and began taking over the pubs. Shop windows were smashed all over the town, cars were vandalised. It was havoc. The local police struggled to cope. These organised firms do run away when they see a police uniform. Many are just likely to stand their ground and have a fight with uniformed officers. The Kenilworth Stand was reserved for away supporters. By 7pm it was overflowing with spectators perched on the scoreboard supports and the turnstiles had been broken. There was no holding them back. Just a few minutes later the police were helpless to stop the hundreds of Millwall supporters scaling the fences in front of the stands and rushing down the pitch towards Luton's supporters in the packed Oak Road End. There was a hail of bottles, cans, nails and coins which had the home supporters fleeing up the terraces but with numbers growing as fans entered the stand, meant that there was little they could do to avoid the missiles. The players came out to warm up and almost immediately vanished back up the tunnel. The Millwall hooligans then set upon the Bobbers Stand, ripping out seats and brandishing them as weapons. A message was put on the electronic scoreboard stating that the match wouldn't start until fans returned to their allotted area, but that was just completely ignored. It was only when the Millwall manager appeared on the side-line that the hooligans returned to the Kenilworth Stand. More reinforcements were called in including police dogs. When the final whistle blew with a 1-0 victory to Luton the Millwall hooligans invaded the pitch. Players from both Millwall and Luton sprinted off the pitch and down into the dressing rooms. The hooligans once more rushed the Bobbers Stand and tore up seats and the fences at the front of the stand were beaten down. The seats were hurled onto the pitch at the police, we were beaten back before re-grouping and rushing forward with batons drawn. I don't think a single officer was shocked when instead of running the fans just stood with their arms outstretched and beckoned them on. The hooligans gathered up the seats and other objects and hurled them at the officers. Several police dog handlers ran forward but were met by hooligans kicking and punching both the officers and the dogs. One officer, Sergeant Colin Cooke, was caught in the centre circle and struck on the head with a concrete block. The officer stopped breathing, but PC Phil Evans resuscitated him while being punched and kicked and then was hit himself by concrete. The carnage continued throughout the town between the Millwall hooligans, the police and surprisingly other football firms who were later identified as Chelsea and West Ham United. Once the mayhem subsided leaving a wake of smashed windows, homes, shops and cars, Luton was brought back under control. There were eighty-one injuries of which thirty-one were police officers and just thirty-one arrests."

"Are we expecting Millwall then sergeant, or an invasion of that scale?"

"No, Millwall are one of many very violent firms. Cardiff have their own firm, the Soul Crew, who have also been building up quite a reputation for violence. Our intelligence suggests that you have your own hooligan firm here. There's quite an anti- league hate for Cardiff, Newport and Swansea. So much so that somebody, we don't know who yet, has managed to pull together the smaller Exeter City firms, that's the H-Troop and The Tea Stand Crew. The latter are named after where they situate themselves at the Cow Shed, closest to the away end at St James Park Stadium. These individuals have been pulled together along with other street gangs from the council estates to form The Sly Crew, who I believe operate from The Vault Pub. The council estate gangs previously had little interest in football but enjoyed regular fights with the marines. Together we're told they have now a hardcore of sixty to eighty lads and they're looking to make a name for themselves. Just like every other firm in the country, especially after Luton, they all want to outdo the others and build their reputation as the top firm. The Soul Crew have a national reputation and have engaged Millwall, Chelsea, West Ham, Tottenham, Portsmouth and Birmingham. They are on the way up. It would suggest that this is an ideal opportunity for a new firm to make a name for themselves and gain recognition on a national scale."

"Sergeant, do we have officer's undercover at Cardiff?"

"I can't say."

"What can we do Sergeant?"

"You do as you always do, you police and keep your eyes peeled. We ignore the obvious looking louts. The top boys, that's those who actively seek out violence with other football firms will be wearing designer sports clothes, smart haircuts. They will look affluent and appear innocent. Those are your targets."

"Do we have an more intelligence Sergeant, like when or where any trouble is likely to take place?"

"'No, at this point we have good reason to believe The Sly Crew will try something. What we need to be is ready to manage and contain any outbursts of violence. So, keep your radios handy and when it starts, you race there as if your life depended on it. Our superiors and the PM will not accept another Luton situation again. It cannot and will not happen."

"Sergeant is it common that rival clubs join forces? From what you've described there seems a clear rivalry, almost hostility from one club to another and yet the London teams, West Ham and Chelsea joined forces with Millwall," said Lucy taking a sip from her tea.

"That's a good question, what was your name?"

"WPC Lucy Penfold Sergeant."

"Yes, that's a very good question. It was something that we haven't seen before. We can only assume that the real target for the day was not Luton's own small hooligan firm, The Migs, but us, the police. A direct attack on the establishment. A show of force. It is no small feat to bring together an army of ten thousand hardcore, battle-ready, hooligans, slide under the transport police's radar, wreak frenzied violence on massive scale and then disappear into the night."

"Do we think it's politically motivated Sergeant?" quizzed Lucy.

The Sergeant smiled.

"No, we don't think so WPC Penfold. What we do have is very clever, violent, men travelling the country with like-minded people whose clear purpose is to engage in acts of violence. The resources are in place, the intelligence is now far superior and the powers that be will make examples of those leading figures or Top Boys as they're known, who are caught, with hefty prison sentences."

***

The following day Lucy was teamed up with Bob. They took the panda car and went out patrolling the area.

"What did you make of all that hooligan firm stuff yesterday?"

"Scary Bob, the fact that these people can organise themselves with military precision around the country is scary. What really concerned me was how instead of the hooligans running when they were charged at by the police they just stood there and fought them with fists, weapons and that one poor guy battered by a concrete block. Sergeant Anderson was right, this is something on a scale we've never encountered before. I'm just surprised that they believe it could happen here in Exeter. I mean in the major cities like London. Birmingham or Manchester it's not hard to accept but Exeter in Devon?"

"I know, at one point I thought you'd hear a pin drop it was so quiet. So, what's the plan Lucy?"

"I thought we'd drive around key locations and keep an eye on what's going on. If we witness anything vaguely suspicious then we radio it in."

"Sounds good. By the way I was sorry to hear about you and Pippa."

"What! How did you hear about that?"

"I just overheard someone and just thought I'd say sorry to hear that things didn't work out."

"Bob, it's not something I really want to discuss. Pippa is yesterday's news now. I've moved on and I believe she has too. So, thank you for your concern but the matter is closed okay?"

"Yeah, sure Lucy I was just, well you know." "Okay, no problem."

Lucy drove by the Harlequin Shopping Centre. She remembered it being The Paul Street Bus Station back in 1982 before it was demolished. There was no unusual activity. As she drove up to the ABC Cinema she found herself thinking how she had watched A View to a Kill, the James Bond Movie, there with Pippa, and how they messed around, with Pippa always able to make her laugh. Lucy remembered how on the 9th December 1980, the night after John Lennon's murder, fans had gathered outside to mourn his death. Next came the Northcott Theatre. It was only last year that she and Pippa had gone to see Alan Ayckbourn's production of Taking Steps. They had both enjoyed it immensely and had talked about it for days after. There did seem to be some activity at The Ship Inn in St Martins Lane. A growing number of smart young men were drinking outside. She asked Bob to radio it in.

Lucy stopped outside The Riverside Leisure Centre. It wasn't even a year ago that she been there at the official opening with Diana, Princess of Wales. Lucy had watched as Diana pressed a button that turned on the pool area including the flume. The Princess tried her hand, albeit very badly, at snooker before being whisked off for lunch at the Guildhall. Lucy had then joined her colleagues as the pageant depicted one hundred and fifty years of policing. She and her colleagues marched down the High Street. Lucy remembered what a truly lovely person Diana, Princess of Wales was.

They drove the car by The Coachmakers Arms. It was heaving with Cardiff Fans. There were two coaches parked close by. Bob radioed it in. They had the visiting targets. Lucy drove quickly to The Queens Vault pub in Gady street. The pub was jam-packed with Exeter City fans. Bob recognised a few of the colourful characters outside drinking, from previous skirmishes with the trainee marines. One of the lads, having spotted them, shot a wanker gesture with his right hand.

"Looks like we know where both sets of fans are so with good policing we should alright."

"I don't believe it'll happen before the match Bob. If it happens it will be after."

***

They drove the car to St James Park Football Stadium and took up their positions along with scores of other officers. They positioned themselves as a natural barrier between the opposing fans as they filed down towards the stadium to gain entry. Lucy watched a few verbal remarks and a couple of V signs, but no real threat. She began to think, and maybe hope, that all that Sergeant Anderson had told them was limited to the big cities and not Exeter. All the fans were inside, the police were well positioned to manage trouble if it happened.

"Have you ever been to a football match Lucy," asked Bob lighting a cigarette?

"No, never. It's never appealed to me. What about you?"

"I don't actually support a team or anything, but when the World Cup is on I do find myself getting quite nationalistic. Normally me and a few lads will get together and find a pub with a TV and we just consume vast amounts of alcohol, get merry and talk bollocks about what we'd do if we get through and then, as always, England play a right shitty game and let the whole country down."

"Could you imagine what it must have been like at Luton in 1985?"

"Lucy, I would insist on a firearm if even half of what Sergeant Anderson said was true."

"Must have been exciting though, you know being on the front line in a real live almost war like situation," said Lucy with a broad grin.

"You, Lucy Penfold, are a bloody nutter. I could just imagine you yelling, screaming and running full on into the thick of it."

Lucy laughed out loud. "It must tell yourself a lot about the kind of person you really are. You know, not in the uniform but who and what you're made of. I suppose the football hooligans must feel the same. When they see their mates running away from us or opposing fans and they're just standing there, outnumbered but ready and willing to fight. They must leave the experience with an incredible sense of self confidence and of course respect from others in their firm."

"Frankly I'd like to see them all rounded up and sent away with long prison sentences."

"Oh, they are definitely breaking the law and there will almost certainly be consequences but then they know it. If you just stop and think about this, even for a few moments, are not these young men showing the same sense of blind loyalty bolstered by the need to fight for their club that our own soldiers did in World War 1?"

"No, definitely not. These people are hooligans fighting for a set of colours, a football club who doesn't even know who they are."

"So, what's the difference between them and a soldier who fights for a Union Jack? A man sent to war to fight people he doesn't know or have ever come into contact with? All he knows is what the politicians tell him. These people are bad, you have to go and fight them."

"What, are you saying that these hooligans that smash up people and property are somehow misunderstood?"

"What I'm saying Bob, if you can open your mind to it for a while. Is that during World War 1 eight hundred and eighty thousand British men died and over two hundred thousand from the Empire. These working-class men were sent to trenches that were wet, cold and exposed to the enemy. When the captain said fix bayonets, they did so without question and when the order came to go over the top and face machine guns they ran towards the enemy. What I'm saying is the football hooligans appear to have the same qualities that those brave soldiers had. Now, because there are no wars, some working-class men have become almost territorial over a football club in an area that some of them don't even live in. I'm not saying it's right, far from it. I'd nick them along with anyone else who broke the law. But when you sit back and analyse the characteristics, then they are, in my opinion, not that far apart."

"Interesting Lucy, I still say lock the bastards up and throw away the key."

"Wait until we find ourselves in another war. As always Bob it nice debating these things with you," said Lucy sarcastically.

Bob reached for the radio.

"I've just heard that Exeter City lost two-nil to Cardiff. I expect tensions will be on the rise. We'd better go and take up our positions. Maybe find a trench somewhere Lucy, fill it with water and wait for the Inspector to give the order to go over the top and nick the hooligans."

"Fuck off Bob!" sneered Lucy!

Lucy drove back towards the Coachmakers Arms. Within minutes they saw a large number of Cardiff fans. Some of them carried crates of beer. The officers watched as they climbed on the two coaches. The last fan climbed on board and both coaches began to pull away. Lucy started the car and stayed a couple of car lengths behind them. Her plan was to escort the coaches to the edge of town and return.

Suddenly, she spotted a brick being thrown at the coach. Then another and another. Both coaches stopped as a car screeched across the road to block them off. Two lads got out and ran through an alley. The coaches were unable to move. They couldn't go forward or reverse. Lucy heard chanting, it got louder and louder "Sly Crew… Sly Crew …. Sly Crew." Scores of young men came from every angle. They were picking up bricks and rocks from the side of the road and hurling them at the coaches. The windows cracked, and broke before caving in. The barrage was relentless. Lucy concluded that during the match a few of the Exeter lads must have placed these bricks and rocks in readiness. The coach doors opened, and a few Cardiff lads managed to get out, but they were outnumbered and battered mercilessly. It was clever, very clever. Despite the larger Cardiff numbers, they were being funnelled down to a single door on a coach. Those that did manage to get out were quickly beaten and battered. Some lay unconscious in a pool of blood. Officers raced to the scene, but the hit was over. The Sly Crew had attacked and strategically beaten the bigger, more notorious club. It would be news that would carry their name and reputation right across the UK. Exeter's Sly Crew were now an established hooligan firm.

Lucy and Bob left the car to join the other officers, but the Exeter hooligans had disappeared as quickly as they arrived. There were no arrests that day and only speculation as to who was involved. In the weeks that followed the police launched operation 'Coddid Offside.' After several months of investigation, a robbery suspect offered up forty of the Sly Crew in exchange for his charges to be dropped.

Chapter 33

"**W**hat are you gift wrapping Lucy?"

"This, Pauline, is a bottle of very expensive Martinho 1881 Vintage Port. I'm sending it to Sergeant Archer. The officer who did my appraisal last year. We had our one-to-one session where he asked me what my goals were for the next twelve months. I told him that after so long in The Murder Squad that I felt de-skilled in normal policing and these were my objectives:

* I want to be a qualified tutor constable and teach others.

* Become an incident car driver.

* Pass Sergeant's exam.

* Promoted to substantive Sergeant within twelve months.

"What you really said all that?"

"That's exactly what he said. He then asked me if I knew about

S.M.A.R.T. to which I replied of course. A specific goal has a much greater chance of being accomplished when it's Specific, Measurable, Attainable, Realistic and Timely."

"What's that then Lucy? I've not heard of it before."

"Sorry Pauline, it's a methodology to ensure that a person achieves the goals they set. They've been widely used in industry for some time and was only recently brought into the police force."

"I bet that surprised him?"

"It did. I told him that that I'd already passed the standard car test so was eligible for the Incident Car Drivers position. But he was having none of it saying that he wasn't going to put a 'girlie' on incident in his lifetime. He then told me the chances of me passing my Sergeant's exam after so long away from mainstream policing would never happen stating that it had taken him six years to pass. I was told that he would not write them down on my notes and that I should reconsider what is truly realistic and achievable again."

"It must have been like talking to a dinosaur!"

"It was. I do understand that what I'd set was a tall order but it I had to tell him that we were not talking about what he could or could not achieve and that we were talking about me. He had no idea of what I'm capable of and to please write my set objectives into my review."

"I bet he wasn't happy with that."

"Pauline he just said that people would laugh but if that's what I want then so be it."

"So how did you do?" Lucy smiled broadly.

'Well I did the incident car and the tutoring and then five days before the twelve months was up I passed my Sergeant's exam, first time, and was promoted to Substantive Sergeant. So, that was all five of my SMART objectives achieved and that's why I'm sending Sergeant Archer this very nice, expensive bottle of Port with a label with 'Who's SMART now – Happy Anniversary.'"

"Lucy, that is so naughty. I love it."

"Another glass of wine?"

"Yes, cheers Pauline and thank you for coming over," said Lucy with her demeanour changing.

"We're friends Lucy and I could tell by the phone call that something wasn't right."

"I think everything has just been catching up and closing in on me. I'm not always thinking straight. A couple of days ago I was sent out to a road accident. Nothing new in that. When I arrived on the scene I saw the car had been slammed hard into a concrete barrier. The front was all stove in and the windscreen was smashed. There was glass everywhere. I looked around the car for the driver. The door was still closed with no sign anywhere. My first thoughts were that it must have been a joyrider who maybe stole the car and when he crashed ran off, so he wouldn't be caught. It was only as I sat back in the panda car that I looked up and there, hanging on a branch was a body."

"Oh my god, that must have been awful."

"Can you imagine if I had left the scene leaving a body hanging in a tree for members of the public. Even worse children on their way back from school. No, this was a wake-up call Pauline. My head has not been in the present, the here and now. Instead I've been quietly consumed over the break up with Pippa."

"'I'm so sorry Lucy," whispered Pauline.

"When I think about it Pauline, the first few months just left me in shock. I put on a brave face but after she casually admitted that she'd been seeing other people I was engulfed with pain. I tried desperately to take control of my emotions and steer myself back from the abyss. There were times, lonely times when I sat in the dark and thought that maybe I should try and get her back. I ran through how it could be done over and over in my head. I played out romance, sex, long discussions, crying and pleading scenarios. I can't believe I even considered allowing her to continue to use me as a fall back when she wasn't playing away. In my hearts heart I knew that she wasn't fully honest with me or completely invested in our relationship. There were quiet times Pauline, when fear and anger took over. Not for long but the feelings were there," said Lucy pausing briefly to take a long sip from her glass.

"I could feel myself stepping away from people. Spending more time on my own. In some strange and stupid way, I still held out hope for an us. I would reflect on how we first got together and convince myself that the love we had was special, a foundation that was strong enough to weather the storm. I even began taking a more philosophical approach, a pragmatic outlook. This was just a blip in our relationship. She said that she loved me and that these girls were nothing more than playthings. I even questioned myself as to what more proof did I need. But, the more I suppressed my anger, hurt and disappointment, the greater those feelings became. As much as these thoughts hurt I had to let them run their course. It did take a while but, I started to acknowledge that I had been deeply wounded and only time would heal it."

"I knew you were in pain Lucy, but I never realised just how much."

"That's okay Pauline, you've been a truly wonderful friend. This was my journey and something that only I could deal with. Eventually I did regain my confidence, I put my foot down and told myself to stop being foolish and pining over Pippa. I started exercising more, I trimmed down, going out and meeting new people. I looked deep into myself and sought the truth and for the most part I liked what I saw. It was then that I found little notes left in my locker, or in the car before going on patrol."

"Little notes?"

"Yeah little notes saying, 'I still love you'. So, in one breath I'm getting these messages, to which I didn't respond, and the next thing I hear that she's been calling me a thief. Telling people that I stole things from her and I swear that there were times when I thought she was following me around. I'd turn my head and briefly catch a glimpse of a person who I'd have sworn was her."

"I hate it when people tell outright lies. It must have been hard cutting off mutual friends."

"It was Pauline, I mean really hard because they were good friends. I just felt that it was important to avoid contact. I wanted and needed to avoid confusion, being hurt and allowing things to get ugly. I know that Pippa wanted to talk but I couldn't allow that to happen no matter how hard the inner conflict was. Do you know I haven't eaten Italian food in bloody ages? It's a place that I associate to us and I couldn't risk going just in case she was there. I worked overtime to keep myself busy, the extra money was nice because I managed to drop a dress size and treated myself to a new wardrobe of clothes."

"Lucy, it really paid off because you look fantastic and those curves girl. You are kicking it."

"Thanks Pauline," said Lucy running a finger through her hair.

"I feel a lot more confident now. No more intense feelings of loneliness, isolation or even fearful of a new relationship. I was angry at myself for feeling so vulnerable."

"Well you've done the right thing now."

"I think I have. A few days ago, I applied for a transfer to Sussex. I needed a new chapter in my life and the body in the tree incident just made change a priority. I was at the nick and walking towards the panda car ready to go on patrol when for the first time in a long while Pippa spoke to me."

"Oh no, what did she have to say?"

"The smell of her perfume was almost over-powering, but I pulled myself together. She told me that after the split she just hated me and when she saw my car parked in the town she just wanted to slash my tyres and scrape her key along the paintwork. She said that she had followed me and had stood in the doorway of the flats opposite my home hoping to catch a glimpse. Pauline, I was stunned. I kept cool and just told her that we were over and that it was fun while it lasted and that I held no grudges and had moved on. It was then that I told her I had transferred to Sussex."

"How did she take that?"

"Her face changed, Pauline, it transformed into a look of utter contempt, hate and evil. She stepped forward with her fists clenched, her face just inches from mine, hissing in a kind of fiery rage that it wasn't over, that I'd never find again what we had, that I would pay, and she would hunt me down and make the rest of my life a fucking misery."

"That's terrible Lucy, dangerous, psychotic criminal behaviour from a police officer. Are you definitely going to Sussex?"

"Yes, but I've heard that Pippa has also requested a transfer!"

Books by Jayne Gooding

The Thick Blue Line

The Thick Blue Line II

The Thick Blue Line III

For Further Information Follow Jayne Gooding Author on Facebook

Printed in Great Britain
by Amazon